WONDERLAND

J. SCOTT COATSWORTH

Published by
Other Worlds Ink
PO Box 19341, Sacramento, CA 95819

FOREWORD

"Wonderland" was first written for a Mischief Corner Books anthology "This Wish Tonight," and was supposed to revolve around a Christmas wish.

Of course, I have a really hard time just writing "plain" contemporary stories, so I had to cast mine in the shadow of the zombie apocalypse. This necessitated a lot of thought over how one might manage in the absence of society, fresh food and international supply chains.

To make things a little harder, I decided to include a character with OCD, which meant another deep dive into the research rabbit hole that is the internet.

I also had a ton of help on this one to get the details right. My deep and abiding thanks to my beta readers: Bellora Quinn, Andrew Kelly, Jon Keys, Ben Brock and Rory Ni Coileain. And a big thank you to Mischief Corner Books, specifically Angel Martinez and Freddy McKay, for both inspiring the story and helping me hone it in edits. Finally, thanks to Donna Kelly, my dear friend who copy-edited this second edition and caught my myriad errors.

This edition has been re-edited, but is essentially the same story as the original.

I'm excited to have Wonderland out again in time for Christmas. Somehow a zombie apocalypse holiday tale seems perfectly appropriate to the dumpster fire of a year that 2020 has been.

Enjoy!

1

____

December 19

Zeke stared up at the darkening sky from the porch of his log cabin. The clouds were rolling in over the mountains, thick as cotton. A year and four months he'd been here all alone, since he'd last seen another living human being. At forty-eight, he was resigned to the fact that nothing in his life was likely to change.

A good storm was coming—he felt it in his bones, although the winter had been unusually warm and dry so far. He'd need to haul some firewood inside the cabin and check his food stocks. He scratched at his scraggly beard, and then carried in the chopped wood to lay it next to the fireplace where some trout he'd fished out of the Clark Fork River was curing, filling the cabin with a heavenly smell.

The supply of canned goods from the local Grocery Surplus store was starting to wear thin, at least all the edible stuff. There was still plenty of canned Brussels sprouts and spinach.

Winter was just beginning—and still not an inch of snow, though that looked like it might change quickly. He stepped back outside and sniffed the chilly air. It smelled like snow, that undefinable crisp, wet scent he used to wait for as a child, ready to charge out into the yard with his brother to throw snowballs and sled down the hillside next to the old church.

Sometimes he wished that he wasn't the last man on Earth. He'd always been a loner—he'd lived up here on the western slopes of the Reservation Divide his whole life, first with his father and brother, and then these last ten years by himself. He'd acted on his impulses once or twice, driving down to Missoula for some big-city life in the town's two gay bars, but he'd never found what he was looking for. Now it was too late. Of course, that reticence had probably saved his life.

It turned out that absence really did make the heart grow fonder. Zeke wished that he had someone—anyone—to talk to.

He snorted. If wishes were fishes, we'd all live in the sea—one of his father's favorite sayings. *Maybe I should think about heading south.*

The first year after the plague, he'd stayed put as it ravaged the big cities on the coasts, and then had made its way inland. Thompson Falls, down in the valley below, had made it a week before the first cases, and then had gone dark in a matter of days.

Even rural Montana hadn't been far enough from civilization to escape the plague's reach.

Even so, he'd run into one of the *besotted,* still living a couple weeks after the End, and had blown the twisted, inhuman thing away with his rifle. Its blood had splattered all over his face, but he hadn't gotten sick.

He grunted. *Someone had to be immune. Maybe I'm the unlucky sod.*

Zeke covered the rest of the wood with a new waterproof tarp to keep out the snow and sleet. That was one advantage of being the last man in the world—there were so many *things* at his disposal, right there for the taking, and he didn't have to pay a dime for them.

Zeke snorted again. Money—such a strange, strange thing. Sometimes he would crack open a cash register in town to grab a handful of metal coins—quarters, dimes, nickels, and pennies—just to run them through his hands and remember the lost world they represented.

He cranked up the generator out back and went into his library room to check the shortwave radio, just like he'd done every day since the plague. It was his ritual, though he'd long since given up hope of hearing from another person.

He sat down and scanned through the bands, listening intently for anything signifying human contact. There was only static.

Zeke went back outside and sniffed the air again. Cold wind whipped at his beard. Snow was coming, for sure, but he should have enough time to make it down to the market for a quick supply run before the storm began.

He checked the fuel gauge on his ATV. It was low—he should probably top off in town and bring some more gas up for his stores. The first month after the plague, when he'd deemed it safe again to go out, he'd found a way to tap the underground tanks at the old Sinclair gas station, so he had all the fuel he needed.

Zeke strapped one of his heavy-duty canvas sacks and an empty gas tank onto the back of the vehicle and hopped on, firing her up. He took a deep breath of the cool, pine-scented air and then started off down the canyon toward the empty town of Thompson Falls.

~

ZEKE REMOVED the board that kept the Grocery Surplus doors closed and pushed them open. He always barricaded it when he left to keep out animal intruders. One time early on, he'd startled a bear inside, licking up honey off the floor. It had given him quite a scare before it lumbered past him and out of the store.

Out back, four makeshift wooden crosses marked the plots where he'd buried Redd Johnson, the owner, and the three others he'd found dead inside.

The checkout counters were covered in a heavy layer of dust he'd never bothered to clean. The plastic grocery sacks had hardened and flaked into little piles of white that swirled like snowflakes whenever the wind blew in from outside.

He picked up one of the faded cardboard boxes that used to hold Hershey bars. They were long gone. He had eaten *a lot* of chocolate in the first twelve months.

The store was out of most of the good stuff now, taken in the initial panic or used by Zeke. It was down to cans of the aforementioned Brussels sprouts and spinach, as well as green beans, canned tomatoes, and Dole fruit salad. Just another indication it was time to move on.

One corner of the ceiling had caved in since the last time he'd been there. He approached the pile of debris in the produce section of the store cautiously. The fruits and vegetables had long since rotted away.

He looked up at the new damage. The hole didn't go all the way through to the roof, just through the interior ceiling. A couple boxes lay crumpled on the ground.

With a leery glance at the broken edges—must have been some kind of storage up there—he opened one of the boxes to see what was inside. It was a disassembled Christmas tree, probably for holiday displays.

Christmas. It had been a long time since he'd celebrated that holiday—or any of them, for that matter—not since his mother had passed away when he was ten. She had owned a tree just like this and had put it up every year. She'd been an environmentalist, not wanting to kill a living thing just to celebrate a man-made holiday.

Zeke glared at the tree and grunted. It wasn't like he needed any more crap in his little cabin.

He closed his eyes, and he could still see her face, lit by the glow of the Christmas lights. "It's the one time of the year when we all have to be nice to each other," she'd whispered to him once, shooting a glance at his father, asleep in his easy chair. Zeke could still smell her sweet perfume. His father had been a rough man. Rough but fair.

"What the hell." He hauled the box out to the ATV and transferred the metal branches into his sack. Then he went back inside to collect some of the remaining food supplies. He cleared out the green bean shelf, grimacing at the thought. He also took the fruit salad. He could always do some hunting to augment his thinning supplies once the storm had passed, or head down the road to Plains. There was a Walmart down in Missoula, but that was a two-hour trek by truck. He'd have to get one of the old beasts running again for such a long trek in the spring, after the snow melted.

He gathered up his supplies and took one last look around the old store.

He used to come to Thompson Falls once a week for groceries. Once. The Surplus had been full of life and light and small-town intrigue. There had been this cute bag boy, just a couple of years younger than him at the time... Davis? Davis Marks. That was it. Tall, close-cropped dark hair, and the most amazing blue eyes young Zeke had ever seen. The guy had been a total flirt too. Zeke still remembered watching his strong, muscular arms, covered in dark hair, as he bagged Zeke's groceries.

Zeke had been way too shy and closeted to make a move or even to say more than a mumbled *thanks*. He regretted that now that there was no one left to make a move on.

He wondered if the bag boy was one of the bodies he'd buried behind the store. It had been impossible to tell.

He tied the sack of supplies to the back of the ATV and headed down the road to the Sinclair gas station, its dinosaur logo a perfect metaphor. He'd spent a whole day, more than a year earlier, disassembling one of the station's two gas pumps to find the dispenser pipe that led down to the tank below.

The first time he'd siphoned off some gas from the tank, it had taken a long time. He'd had to blow enough air into the tank through one tube to increase the air pressure enough to force some of the gasoline up the other, a process akin to filling up a hundred air mattresses with his own lungs.

Once he'd managed it though, he had filled up the gas-powered pump he'd found at the True Value hardware store, and he'd been off and running. Now he left everything in place, covered by a tarp and some rocks to protect it from the weather. It was almost as convenient as filling up at the station had been before the plague. Plus he didn't have to pay.

A skull stared at him from across the pavement. Zeke turned away, looking up at the gray sky. He'd learned to ignore the corpses of the rest of the naked dead that lay scattered about town. They were slowly rotting away into dust, or being torn apart by roving dogs and wolves. In another year or two, it would be like they'd never been there at all.

"Dammit!" he cursed as the gas overflowed the ATV's tank and splattered all over him. He'd let himself get distracted.

He sighed. He'd given up *being presentable* months before. He was lucky to manage a bath once a month these days.

A couple of dogs from the local pack—a Samoyed and a poodle mix gone feral—were sniffing in his direction. He'd considered shooting one or two for the meat, but dogs were pets, not food, even if these acted more like wild hunters. That was ingrained in him since birth, but if he got really hungry, it might have to change. He picked up a chunk of loose pavement and threw it at them, scattering them.

He filled up the two gas cans he'd brought with him from the cabin.

A snarl brought him around. The pack was back, and had grown to five. They looked hungry. The dogs advanced on him, a motley bunch that included a Doberman and a dachshund pulling up the rear like a little caboose.

Zeke reached for his rifle and pumped a bullet into the chamber. Usually that was enough to scare off the curs. This time though, the Doberman continued to advance, snarling.

Zeke sighed. He shot the gun into the air, the sound reverberating around him.

The dogs yelped, turned tail, and ran.

They were becoming less and less afraid of him. *That's a bad sign.* He might be eating dog meat for Christmas after all.

Zeke put the rifle away and saddled up. The air was getting colder, the wind blowing in his face and running its fingers through his long hair, and the clouds had completely blocked out the sun. He set off up the dirt road into the hills, toward the cabin.

The first flakes of snow were falling when Zeke pulled up in front of his home. Vermilion Peak loomed over the little valley, still green this late in the year. By midnight it would be mantled in white.

He lifted the garage door manually and pulled the ATV inside, and as a wind gust blew the recently fallen flakes around, he pulled the door back down to block out the storm.

He checked his Fish of the Month calendar. December was trout month. The days of the week were all off, now since it was the previous year's version, but each day he marked off another one so he could keep track of the actual date. Whether it was Sunday or Thursday had ceased to have significance, now that there were no more churches, no more work weeks, and no more TV schedules to follow.

December 21, the winter solstice, was just two days away.

He put away his booty on the wooden shelves in the garage that his father had built decades earlier. The gasoline and the Christmas tree went in one corner, and he took a can of green beans and a can of fruit salad inside.

His cabin was a small place—garage, kitchen, living room, bathroom, one bedroom downstairs, and two bedrooms and another bath upstairs that he'd converted to storage. It was all he really needed. His father and mother had shared the large upstairs bedroom until she had passed away from cancer when he was little. Zeke's father had died a couple of decades later, crushed by a car he'd been fixing.

After that, Zeke had been all alone.

Now he slept in the master bedroom and used the smaller one upstairs for his books. The downstairs room—the guestroom— hadn't seen a guest since his brother had come home to visit ten years before.

The familiar pain squeezed his chest. Jerod was dead and gone, but knowing it didn't make it any easier to stomach.

Zeke had saved the entire science fiction and fantasy section from the public library, which in Thompson Falls amounted to a couple hundred titles, heavy on Golden Age sci-fi. Many of them were first editions, printed in the 40s and 50s. Not that it mattered anymore.

He settled in with a copy of *Rendezvous with Rama,* one of his favorite Clarke books, as the snow came down more heavily outside and the winds howled like hungry wolves.

NATHAN TRUDGED SLOWLY up State Highway 200. The sign by the side of the road read, "Welcome to Thompson Falls, Home of Western Hospitality."

Above, snow clouds were massing.

He should have stayed back in Missoula. It was a small place as far as big cities went, but still one of the larger towns he'd walked through on his journey from Vermont since leaving Fargo. The weather had been so good though, and he was eager to finish his journey back to Vancouver.

At his side, Andy whistled a merry tune.

It had been more than a year since they'd set out—since the plague had cast Nathan loose from his moorings. He'd been at a gay summer camp up in Vermont when it struck, and he'd been the only survivor.

When he'd reached Rutland, he'd realized that the plague hadn't been isolated to the little campground. It had happened all across Vermont, the States, the world—even back home in Vancouver.

He'd had a run-in with some of the infected who were still alive as he'd gotten close to town. They'd scared the bejesus out of him: two men naked and aroused, with a look in their eyes that would haunt him until the day he died, full of hunger and lust, pain and death. He'd barely escaped with his life, and then only because he'd been a championship runner in school.

He'd soon discovered that driving the roads was useless. There were far too many wrecks, especially near the cities. It was best to stay away from large urban centers, in any case. So he'd found an abandoned gas station and liberated a map, then set off on foot across the Vermont countryside.

He just wanted to get home.

"It's pretty here," Andy said, glancing appreciatively at the mountain peaks that lined either side of the road.

Nathan nodded. It was cool out, but he was warm enough with his sweatshirt and long johns under his jeans. His backpacker's pack was stuffed full of clothes and food supplies, along with his sleeping bag and tent. "It's gonna snow soon though. We should probably find shelter." Nathan didn't remember anymore when or where he'd met Andy—outside of Buffalo maybe? It seemed like he'd always been there, but then again, the hundreds of days on the road had blurred together. Having a traveling companion had made the journey much easier, though Andy didn't ever do much more than talk.

Andy pointed at the sign. "I'm sure we can find a place to hole up there."

"Some place *simple*." The less there was to deal with, the better. Nathan's compulsions had eased on the road, but whenever he was in a house or human-built structure, any place where *things* were stacked on *things*, they returned, along with the idea that *it wasn't safe*. He'd taught himself through more than a decade of therapy to minimize the effect his OCD had on his life, but it would always be a part of him.

Andy nodded.

There was a sharp crack in the distance up ahead.

"Was that a gunshot?" *Holy shit.* Andy was the only other plague survivor he'd found.

"Sure sounded like it."

"Come on!" Nathan set off at a run down the empty highway, the pack bouncing awkwardly on his back, and Andy followed. Walking every day for fourteen months had put him in the best shape of his life—not bad for a guy in his early forties.

He cleared a rise in the road where he could see a gas station up ahead. As he watched, an ATV roared to life, carrying someone across the highway and along a dirt road, heading up a narrow valley toward the mountains.

"Hey!" he shouted and started running down the highway again after the stranger. "Hey, over here!"

The driver didn't seem to hear him. Nathan ran down the hillside toward the station, but the ATV was soon lost in the distance.

"There's someone else still alive," he said to Andy in wonder, staring after the stranger.

"Um... Nathan?"

Something growled. He turned to find a pack of feral dogs that had appeared at the side of the road. "Shit."

He pulled out his hunting knife. Andy had told him he needed a gun, but Nathan *hated* firearms. He always had. Of course, he'd never really needed one until now.

A skin-and-bones Doberman snarled and leapt at him, teeth bared. Nathan knocked the dog aside with his left arm, stumbling to the side. The animal hit the ground and slid across the pavement before regaining his feet. He could smell the pungent unwashed animal smell of it, ripe like a barn stall.

A tall, lanky poodle mix came at Nathan next, jaws snapping. Nathan hopped backward and stumbled, slipping off the edge of the highway and going down in a heap into the shallow drainage gutter.

"Help me!" he shouted, but Andy was gone. He struggled to his knees, but the dogs were on him before he could get back up.

The Doberman growled and sunk its teeth into his leg, and the pain flared up his thigh.

Nathan slashed wildly at the attacking pack with his knife, eliciting a yelp from the poodle and a terrifying growl from a dirty Samoyed. Blood splashed across his face; theirs or his own, he couldn't tell.

He scrambled back in the gravel and kicked hard. His tennis shoe connected with something, and one of the smaller dogs went flying away with another loud yelp.

Where the hell was Andy?

Pain flared again in Nathan's left arm and leg, pushing him into berserker mode. He was fighting for his life.

He lashed out and cut the Doberman across the throat. It fell to the pavement, gasping and twitching, blood gushing out of the fresh wound.

Then he shoved his knife into the poodle's flank. It screamed and ran away, and the other dogs broke off the attack to run off after it, all except for the Doberman, bleeding out on the pavement.

"You okay?" Andy was standing behind him, a worried frown on his face.

"Where were you?" Nathan looked up at his friend, the cloudy light creating a halo over Andy's head. There wasn't a scratch on him. Nathan hauled himself to his feet.

"I went to look for something to beat them off with." He held up a large stick. "Guess you didn't need my help, after all."

"I really could have used it," Nathan grumbled, checking his wounds. Andy was useless. If it weren't for his companionship, Nathan would have left him behind long before.

His arm wasn't too bad—as long as the dogs didn't have rabies —but his leg had at least one decent bite wound, and he was bleeding. He looked down the road toward the waiting town and across the field where the ATV had gone. There was no telling how far away the stranger lived, but he wasn't about to give up on the first survivor they'd run across, wounded or not.

Nathan shrugged off his pack and pulled out his water bottle, rinsing off the wound. Then he took out a clean shirt, tying it around the leg bite. He secured it tightly, hoping it would slow the bleeding.

Then he stood unsteadily. He took one step, then another, ignoring the pain lancing through his thigh.

Someone else is still alive. He could do this. He *had* to do this.

"You okay to walk?" Andy asked, with a dubious glance at his leg.

"Yeah, I can manage for a bit." He hauled himself, one halting step at a time, across the field toward the road the ATV had taken. "Come on."

Andy followed wordlessly.

Time blurred as they followed the dirt road—more of a track—up into the valley. Stands of birch trees shivered in the wind, their remaining leaves making a sound like a running brook. Tall ponderosa pines dotted the hillsides too, great sentinels watching his passage.

Clouds filled the sky above, falling toward the valley, and the temperature continued to drop.

Step, step, step.

Nathan was tired. He was losing blood-a glance down at the red-soaked shirt confirmed it. He had to concentrate on each individual movement and on the faint road they followed.

At some point, snow started to drift down, falling at first in little friendly flakes. Then it came down more heavily, and he hurried on, straining against the aching of his wound to go as quickly as possible before the snowfall covered the tracks. If the ATV had gone farther than he could walk, he might just have made a fatal mistake.

Andy was at his side, ready to lend a hand, but Nathan didn't ask for one.

After half an hour, he stopped to look back the way they had come. The road and the outskirts of town were gone, vanished behind a hillside. "Maybe we should go back," he said, stopping in his tracks as the snow started to fall more heavily. He was heading into the unknown, and he might well get trapped out here.

"You have to go on," Andy said. "You said it yourself. What if that's the only other guy left on Earth?"

Nathan shook his head. He had *thought* it, not said it... 'Someone else is still alive,' but had he actually said it? He couldn't remember. Pain lanced up from the wound on his leg, but he could handle it. Andy had gotten really good at reading him. His friend was right though. How could he pass up this chance? *I have to keep going.*

They climbed slowly into the hills.

The world dimmed as the storm worsened. The road and the ATV tracks had almost been erased by the falling snow. Nathan had the horrible feeling that they weren't going to make it before the signs vanished altogether.

He shivered, looking around at this quiet place in the mountains, surrounded by pine trees and sweeping peaks. *Not such a bad place to die.* He'd outlasted almost everyone else, after all. *I win!* It was a bitter victory.

"Look!" Andy pointed to something ahead.

There was a glow. Nathan stumbled forward, and a red two-story cabin appeared as if created from whole cloth out of the snowfall, its windows shining with welcoming golden light. Smoke poured from the chimney into the darkening sky. It was like something off a Christmas card.

Nathan's heart beat faster. *It can't be.* What were the odds? That someone besides the two of them had survived all this time? And that his path homeward would bring him so close to this lone survivor?

Andy was grinning. "Come on. What are we waiting for?"

"The grim reaper with his scythe?" Nathan grumbled. Andy was really starting to piss him off.

Andy snorted. "You're not that bad off."

Nathan felt like death frozen over himself, but he decided he could make it another hundred feet. He pulled himself along, dragging his injured leg in the snow.

Step, drag. Step, drag. Another fifty feet to go.

Step, drag. Thirty more feet. Almost there.

He took a deep breath, closing his eyes as colors swirled in his vision amidst the snow and the world seemed to melt.

He shook his head, and the world was right again.

At long last, they reached the porch, which was covered with a dusting of snow. The two steps ahead of him seemed almost insurmountable.

"You can do it," Andy said.

"Go fuck yourself." Nathan sat down on the first step to catch his breath. His leg was on fire, and his fingers and toes were numb.

"Are you *seriously* going to lay down and die, just five feet from his door?"

"*His* door?"

"Their door. Whatever." Nathan's hands were on his hips, his lips pulled up in a look of disgust.

Nathan glared at him. "Why can't you go knock for me?" He was getting really annoyed with Andy. The asshole would probably leave him to die if Nathan gave him half a chance.

"Come on, *Nate*. You can do this. Crawl if you have to."

"It's *Nathan*," he growled, but he managed to turn himself over on his stomach with some effort. He pulled himself across the snow-covered porch like a worm toward the door. Foot by foot, then inch by inch.

At last, he lay there in front of the big green wooden door and reached up to knock on it.

Only then did Andy finally shout, "Open up in there. We need help!"

Nathan knocked again, as hard as he could with the last of his strength. Then he collapsed onto the hard wood planks of the porch.

He looked up blearily at Andy and thought he could the porch roof through his friend's head. *I'm hallucinating.*

Nathan closed his eyes, his face sinking down into the cold drift of snow piled against the doorway. He was done.

THE EXPLORERS from Earth had just landed on the alien ship as it whipped around the sun on its journey to parts unknown.

Clarke really knew how to write 'em. Zeke turned the page, taking a sip of the white wine he'd uncorked that evening. He was still a long way from cleaning out the liquor store. Outside the wind howled.

Knock, knock, knock.

He looked up, perplexed. He hadn't heard a knock on his door in years, even before the plague—part of that whole loner thing, he was sure. It was probably just one of the trees banging its branches against the cabin.

After a moment, he went back to the book. *Now, where was I?*

Knock, knock.

It had sounded more distinct that time, but still...

He set the book and his wine glass down and sprang toward the front door. He pulled the rifle down from its rack just in case and opened the door, certain there would be no one there.

There was a low moan, barely audible above the wind.

Zeke looked down, and it took a moment for his brain to sort out what he saw there.

"Jesus Christ!" It was the prostrate form of a man—or a woman? It was impossible to tell. They lay face down in the snow.

He knelt and put his finger on the person's neck. It was still warm, and there was a pulse. He felt a moment's trepidation… could they be besotted? Unlikely. The plague had burned itself out years before.

Besides, the besotted never knock. He set down the rifle. "Come on," he said, though whoever it was seemed unconscious and unlikely to hear him. "Let's get you inside." He knelt and hooked his arms under the person's armpits and pulled them into the living room, then closed the door to block out the cold. *How do you treat frostbite again? Blankets. I need blankets.*

Zeke pulled off the stranger's backpack and set it aside. He turned the body over carefully.

It was a man, and a good-looking one at that, from what he could see under the snow and grit.

He lay the stranger gently on the thick rug by the fireplace, went to grab a pile of blankets from his closet, and set a few by the open flames to warm up.

Then he set about stripping the stranger down.

Zeke chuckled softly to himself. He'd dreamed of such a moment for years, and here it was. Somehow he'd always imagined it would be under much more romantic circumstances.

Still, his visitor was in good shape. Zeke's hand lingered on his flat stomach for just a moment.

The man's left pant leg was shredded. It looked like he had been bitten, maybe by a wild dog. He'd have to take out that pack, qualms or no. They'd gotten a taste of human flesh, and they'd be twice as aggressive now.

Zeke needed something to cleanse the wounds. He poured some of the hot water from his fireplace kettle into a bowl to cool off. Then he pulled off the man's boots and socks. His feet were rank, but nothing like he would have expected. Hopefully frostbite hadn't set in yet. *Where did you come from, my friend?*

He removed the pants with a pair of shears, leaving the cloth tied in place around the leg wound. The man had four bite marks on his legs and arms, but only the one under the shirt looked severe.

Yup, they were from dog teeth. *That* could be a problem.

One step at a time, ol' Zeke.

He wrapped one of the warmed blankets around the man's feet and covered his lower legs with another. He wrapped another blanket around his chest.

Only the large wound on the man's left thigh was actively bleeding. Zeke grabbed some soap and some bandages he'd scrounged from the Doug's Drug in town. Then he held a bundle of bandaging over the wound for ten minutes until it stopped bleeding.

He used some cool, soapy water to wash out the wounds, paying special attention to the ones on the man's leg. When he'd gotten them as clean as he could manage, he laid a large, clean piece of bandaging over the biggest wound and wrapped more around it to keep it in place. He used another patch on the smaller wound and then turned to tend to the ones on the man's left arm.

It took the better part of an hour, but at last he was satisfied that he'd done all he could. He got out some Vancomycin he had left over, and some Tylenol.

Holding the man's head on his lap, he whispered, "I need you to swallow these. It will help."

The man blinked his eyes open and then closed.

Zeke took that for a sign that he'd been understood. He poured the water slowly into the man's mouth, massaging his throat to help him swallow, like he used to do with the family dog.

After a coughing fit when the water went down the wrong way, the man managed to get the pills down.

Zeke laid him back on the rug, unconscious. Zeke shifted him onto a clean blanket and wrapped him up gently, laying him near the fire to rest. Then he threw the blood-soaked rug out into the snowstorm. He'd get another from town on his next trip.

He took the remaining hot water from the kettle and made himself a cup of Earl Grey tea. There'd only been two boxes left when he'd first raided the store, so he used the tea sparingly, trying to make it last as long as possible. For now, he could scavenge more from other towns, but someday it would all be gone—the tea, the canned food, all the products of the old world. What then? He rarely thought about the future—the present was hard enough to get through. But somehow the stranger's appearance triggered all kinds of strange thoughts in his head.

Zeke sat down in his dad's old threadbare recliner and watched his handsome stranger, asleep in front of the fireplace.

What was he like? Did he like women or men? Zeke let himself fantasize about the man for just a minute. *What if he's gay?* Zeke snorted, bitterly amused with himself. *Wishful thinking.*

Once the shortwave radio had gone dark, he'd made peace with the fact that he was one of the last people left in the world, if not the only one. He'd gone through the last year stocking up, figuring out how to take care of his needs that civilization had once met, planning for a long, lonely life of utter solitude. He'd certainly never encountered another person since.

What if he had been wrong? What if there were *others*?

No sense borrowing trouble. Sooner or later, his guest would wake up, if infection didn't set in and kill him first. Then they could talk.

Zeke looked around the place. It was a mess, with dusty scavenged crap stacked up everywhere. He couldn't remember the last time he'd cleaned the floor.

He was probably ripe himself. Baths were difficult these days, and after a few months, he'd stopped bothering more than monthly.

His visitor was too out of it to care, but when he woke up... Well, it would be nice to not scare the poor man half to death.

Zeke set to work. He started with the downstairs bathroom. He lit a couple candles and wiped the mirror clean with an old bottle of Windex and some paper towels from his stash in the garage. He cleaned the sink and peeked in the tub. It was pretty nasty down there too.

Zeke wet the tub down with rainwater from the barrel in his garage and dumped what was left of a can of Comet in there to soak. He'd need to make a run to the store to pick up some more cleaning products.

The piles of scavenged junk he'd brought into the cabin over the last sixteen months would have to wait.

Then he got a good look at himself in the newly cleaned mirror. He grinned. *I look like a mountain man.* Well, technically he *was.* He resembled that big hairy guy from the Harry Potter films. Zagreb? Hagrid? Only worse. His light brown hair was a tangled mess, both his beard and on his head.

Zeke grabbed his shears and started hacking away at the mess of a beard. It was tangled up in knots and took him a good twenty minutes to trim off the worst of it. He *really* missed electric trimmers. Hell, he missed electricity in general. If there hadn't been a blizzard outside, he could have started up the gas generator. For now, shears would have to do.

At last, he had his beard looking half decent and went after the hair on his head. That was considerably more difficult. He had to reach around to the back to chop off the worst of it, and when he was done, it looked like a deranged stylist had done a hatchet job on his head.

At least it was better than before.

He washed it five times with more rainwater, along with his beard, and was ashamed at how much dirt came out. He really had let himself go.

He glanced out the bathroom door at the man still asleep on his living room floor, feeling a little thrill at the sight.

Then he saw what a mess the house was in. He hoped the guy would sleep for at least a week. It would take him that long to make himself and the cabin presentable.

Outside, the storm roared on.

Zeke made good use of the time. He scrubbed out the tub and then hauled some fresh-fallen snow from his porch in to heat in a bucket over the fire. After a couple hours, he had enough for a decent bath. He settled in and luxuriated in the warm water, opening a new box of Irish Spring soap and scrubbing off months of accumulated dirt.

When he was done, he heated some more water and washed himself down again, making sure he was really clean.

Then he went to work on the rest of the house.

He finished the living room, cleaning around the sleeping body of the stranger and making it moderately presentable, by what he judged to be about midnight. Then he decided it was time to take a break.

He'd put a pillow under his visitor's head and changed the dressing on his wound. He'd even managed to get a couple more antibiotics down the man's throat, and now the stranger was sleeping soundly.

Zeke put a few more logs on the fire. The storm blustered outside, but inside, it was warm and dry, cheery in a way it hadn't been in years.

He lay down on the couch where he could keep an eye on the man. For a long time he couldn't sleep, too excited to find out everything about his new company.

But eventually sheer exhaustion won out, and he fell into a deep, heavy sleep.

2

———

December 20

The storm finally abated the next afternoon, blowing out with a rattling sigh that left things absolutely still and pristine outside the windows. The cabin was looking halfway decent now, at least by comparison, but Zeke was almost out of both cleaning supplies and bandages.

He'd checked the shortwave again first thing in the morning. If there was one other survivor, maybe there were more. *No such luck.* He was greeted only by static and silence.

Zeke also changed the man's bandages. The bite wound on his leg seemed a little red and puffy, but the antibiotics hadn't had much time to work yet. He knelt next to his visitor and whispered, "I gotta run into town now. I'll be back in a couple hours. I'll leave you a note, just in case." Zeke patted the man's shoulder, but his visitor didn't move.

Zeke scribbled out a quick message and then pulled his

snowmobile out of his garage, topped off the fuel tank, and started off toward Thompson Falls.

The hills were covered in white, a good twelve to fourteen inches of snow making the forest into a winter wonderland. It reminded him of the old Perry Como song, and he sang it as he bounced over the hills. He was a passable singer, but he'd always been too embarrassed to sing in public, before.

He missed Christmas music. He missed lots of things. People. Cars. Television. *Oh God, how I miss those Desperate Housewives.*

Most of all, though, he missed simple human contact. It was good to see another living human being, to touch his warm, beautiful skin, even under the circumstances.

To hope the man would touch him back.

The snowmobile kicked up a spray of fresh-fallen snow that shimmered in the afternoon sun. It was chilly out, the first real taste of winter in a season that had been too warm.

After about fifteen minutes, he pulled into town. The buildings were still standing, and the snow had covered what was left of the remains of the prior inhabitants. It almost felt like the before times.

Zeke still wasn't sure how he'd escaped the end of the world.

Some of his shortwave pals had speculated that the virus that caused it had been human engineered. It had appeared almost everywhere at once.

Then, one by one, they dropped off the radio spectrum. Every last one.

He pulled up in front of Doug's Drug and opened the door, sneezing at the dusty air inside. The animals had mostly left this place alone, as there had been little food here.

He grabbed a plastic basket from the stack up front and filled it with more bandages, antiseptic, and cleaning and personal hygiene supplies.

He grabbed a few half-melted candles for good measure and

stuffed them in a bag, tying it to the back of the snowmobile. Then he popped into the True Value store to pick up a replacement rug.

He had one final stop he wanted to make before heading home.

NATHAN OPENED HIS EYES.

He was inside a rustic log room, wrapped up in blankets, next to a fire that had burned down almost to embers.

He pushed off the blankets and sat up. His head swam and his leg pulsed with pain. *Where am I?*

It slowly came back to him—the stranger on the ATV, the attack of the feral dogs, and following the ATV's tracks to a cabin.

Where was the stranger? Had he dreamed that part? And yet here he was in someone's clearly inhabited cabin. "Hello?" he called, but no one answered. *Where's Andy?*

There was a scribbled note taped to the couch next to him. He grabbed it, squinting at the messy handwriting:

I GOTTA RUN into town now. I'll be back in a couple hours. —Zeke

ZEKE.

Nathan looked around. The cabin was clean enough, but it was stuffed to the gills with *stuff*. Things on top of other things. Papers, boxes, household gadgets, piles and piles stacked against walls and in corners. Some of the piles looked dangerously close to falling over. He looked up into the face of a moose head which stared at him though glassy eyes from above the fireplace.

It's not safe.

The thought slipped unbidden into his head like an old friend.

Panic gripped his gut, and he tried to breathe his way through it, laying back down and closed his eyes.

This was someone else's place. He had no right to mess with it.

It's not safe.

He knew that thought, was intimately familiar with its lure. *It's not me*, he told himself. *It's the OCD.*

His old nemesis had been largely silent on his trek across the country. There were few stacks of things to rearrange in the wild, and Andy had helped talk him down when he needed it most.

Andy was gone.

The thought would whisper to him at night, familiar as his own skin, but it didn't scratch at him like it used to. Until now...

It's an irrational thought. It's not *me.*

His therapist had taught him to deal with the fact that a part of his brain was broken. It wasn't his fault. It just was.

Look what he'd done with his life. He'd found successful employment as an insurance adjuster, bought a small condo in downtown Vancouver. He had his shit together. At least until the plague had wiped away the old world.

He'd even walked across more than half of the country. That was an amazing thing.

It's not safe.

He could move past this. It was just his broken brain, not him.

He was exhausted. He must have lost a lot of blood. He needed to sleep.

He focused on his throbbing leg, and slowly, so slowly, the idea faded, just a little. It was still there, but quieter, and he was able to ignore it, for the moment.

After a while, the throbbing eased, and he fell back into a deep sleep.

~

ZEKE ROLLED up to the little cemetery on the eastern edge of town.

The sun was low on the horizon, shining under the roof of clouds, but the storm was over for now. The snow had covered all the grave markers, but he knew where to find the ones he was looking for. He crossed the white field, startling a group of deer searching for buried grass. They bounded off under the trees, then stared at the interloper.

It was their world now.

He found the spot under an old stand of ponderosa pine trees that lined the edge of the cemetery. Brushing off the snow, he uncovered the plaques that marked his mother and father's final resting place, side by side for eternity. He sat back in the snow, staring at the graves, and then looked up at the sky above.

It had been months since he'd come here. There hadn't seemed much point to it really. Nothing had changed in his own life, and it wasn't like his parents were really *there* anyhow.

Not that he believed in the whole afterlife thing. More than likely, they were gone from the world altogether, their stories now only known to him, and when he was gone... *Ashes to ashes and all that.*

Nevertheless, he came here sometimes, just to talk to them.

"I'm sorry it's been so long," he said, staring at the clouds. "I've been kind of drifting. Nothing much to do anymore."

He scratched absently at his elbow, looking at the deer who were edging their way toward him. A generation or two, he supposed, and they'd have no fear of men at all—if there were any men left.

"Something happened today," he said at last. "Someone, actually. I didn't know there was anyone left besides me." He chuckled. "I don't know if I wished him here. That's crazy, right?" He stared at their names, John Evan and Carmen Mary Mitchell.

"Maybe you sent him to me?" It was a crazy thought, but no crazier, really, than the madness the world had descended into with the plague. "Maybe there are others out there too."

He remembered his cousin's kids when they'd come up to visit the cabin one year before his father had passed away. How alive they'd been, laughing and playing hide and seek in the woods behind the house. It would be nice for there to be children in the world again.

He sat there for a while in silence, listening to the wind through the trees and smelling the cool crisp air. It was peaceful, serene, a few moments carved out of his usual survival mode to just breathe.

Until his ass started to get cold from the snow.

"I love you," he whispered. They might not have understood him, but they were his parents, and he missed them still. He kissed his hand and touched each grave marker, lingering for a moment more.

Then he got up and made his way back toward the snowmobile with a nod to the deer.

THE SOUND of an engine rumbling outside the cabin woke Nathan again. He turned over carefully and stared at the door. He was still weak, but the pain in his leg wounds had subsided to a dull ache.

He eased himself into a sitting position and edged over to the couch, where he could prop himself up.

The piles of junk around the room looked all but ready to fall over in a gigantic crash.

It's not safe.

The door swung open, and Nathan was momentarily blinded by the bright light from outside. He put his hand in front of his face, squinting up at the newcomer.

"Hey, you're up!" It was a man's voice. It sounded rough, as if he hadn't used it in a long time. The door closed, and Nathan got a better look at his host.

The man looked to be in his mid-to-late forties, with a close-trimmed beard and short dark hair streaked with bits of gray. He also looked like a mad hair stylist had attacked him in his sleep. Then again, Nathan figured he didn't look much better.

The man was handsome enough, in a rugged way, like the guy on the Bounty paper towel package, red flannel and all. He seemed to be in good shape. "I... yeah, I'm up. You must be Zeke? Thank you for taking me in."

It's not safe.

Nathan closed his eyes. *Leave me alone.* Those words weren't *his.* He didn't have to listen to them. He had done this before, found a way to move past them.

"Hey, you okay?" Zeke put down the sack he was carrying and knelt next to him, concern evident in the fine lines around his eyes.

Nathan sighed. "I will be. I just have this... thing."

"Thing?"

"Sorry. I have OCD. It can be hard to ignore it ,sometimes."

Zeke nodded. "We all have something. I'm Zeke... as you clearly already figured out from the note."

Nathan opened his eyes. "Nathan." He held out his hand.

Zeke shook it. His hand was warm, real. "Nice to meet you, Nate."

He frowned. "It's Nathan. Nobody's called me *Nate* since I was six."

"Fair enough. Nathan, you hungry?" Zeke picked up the bag and headed through a doorway into another room. "Menu's not too impressive, but there's plenty of food."

"Actually... my leg hurts. Do you have any pain meds?"

"Sure. I'll bring you some Tylenol and a couple more

Vancomycin. Can't be too careful with those wounds."

Nathan looked down at his leg. Someone—Zeke, probably—had done a nice job of wrapping it up. That reminded him of the dogs, which reminded him of his traveling companion. "Where's Andy?" he asked Zeke when the man returned with a glass of water and the pills.

"Andy who?"

"The man traveling with me."

"There were two of you?" Zeke sounded surprised. He handed Nathan the pills.

Nathan downed them in two gulps. "Yeah, since... well, at least since Buffalo."

"Damn. I thought I was the only one left." Zeke took back the glass. "Wait. You walked all the way across the country?"

Nathan nodded. "It's taken me more than a year. But I didn't really have anything else to do."

"I know the feeling." Zeke shook his head in admiration. "Don't know what to tell you. There was no one outside but you when I opened the door."

Nathan shook his head. "Andy wouldn't just leave me." He'd done it before though, with the dogs, and if Nathan was honest with himself, there had been other times too.

Zeke put his arms around Nathan gently. "I'm sure he'll come back for you."

Nathan stiffened in Zeke's arms. He felt himself starting to shake. *I'm not ready for this.* He had been alone for so long. He hadn't been touched by another human being in a year.

Andy... well, Andy was probably straight. He'd never wanted to touch Nathan, in any case.

But he was touched by the warmth of Zeke's strong arms and by the way this total stranger had taken care of him.

He glanced at the piles of junk over Zeke's shoulder.

It's not safe.

He shook his head violently, trying to dislodge the insistent voice. *That isn't me. It's the broken part of my brain. It isn't me.*

His therapist had taught him coping mechanisms—how to try to move past it when he got stuck in an OCD loop. His condition had been mostly dormant during his trek across country. But now... "I think I'm okay," he whispered.

Zeke let him go, frowning.

"I don't suppose you have any Xanax?" It had helped him control his compulsions for a short time before.

Zeke shook his head. "Sorry. We can probably get some from town tomorrow."

"That would be good. Thanks." *I can hold it together for a night. Maybe.*

"Let me get some food going. You like fruit salad?"

Nathan wrinkled his nose. "You have anything that's not from a can? I've been eating out of cans for over a year."

Zeke snorted. "I hear that. Well, I have some salmon I caught and smoked. I can plate up some of that with some fruit salad on the side."

Nathan laughed. "Sounds like a grand meal. I'd kill for a nice green salad with vinaigrette."

"Vinaigrette I can do, but salad..." Zeke shrugged. "Hard to garden here in the winter."

"Yeah, I'd imagine." He'd gotten lucky. Zeke seemed like a decent guy.

"I even have a few beers—"

He shook his head. "Better not. Thanks." He'd never cared much for alcohol. Plus it could mess with the meds.

"Fair enough. Give me a couple minutes and I'll whip something up. Sorry the place is a mess. I don't get much... well, any company anymore."

"It's all right."

It's not safe.

Nathan took a deep breath and closed his eyes. *Not me. Bad brain.*

The itch remained, but he refused to scratch it.

ZEKE RETURNED to the kitchen and pulled a couple dirty plates from the sink.

Nathan had *flinched* when Zeke had hugged him. He had started to shake.

Did that mean Nathan liked him? Was afraid of him, disgusted by him? He didn't know how to read the signs. He'd always been crap with all that *touchy feely* stuff.

He glared at the stacks of dirty dishes. He hadn't quite finished cleaning the place, but maybe he could keep Nathan out of there until he had a chance to get things organized.

His visitor seemed like a nice guy. Zeke wished his gaydar was better.

He washed the plates with some dish soap, giving them a good scrub, and dried them with some of his precious paper towels. He pulled out the last of his smoked salmon and put it on the plates, along with the fruit salad. "I have a few Snapples left," he called. "Lemon or peach?"

"Peach is fine."

Zeke hauled the plates and a couple forks out into the living room and presented one of them to Nathan with a flourish. "Compliments of the chef."

Nathan laughed. "What I wouldn't give to go to a nice restaurant again." He took the plate and set it on his lap.

"I would love to have cheese again. Especially mozzarella."

"I would die for a Hershey's Special Dark chocolate bar."

"I loved dark chocolate." Zeke returned with the drinks and a couple more paper towels and took a seat on the floor against the wall by the fireplace where he could see Nathan properly. "Where did you start out on your journey?"

"Vermont. Seems like I've been walking forever." Nathan took a bite of the salmon. "What about you? Ooh, this is delicious."

Zeke looked around the old cabin. *So many memories.* "I grew up here. This was my Dad's place. He passed away a few years ago."

"It's... nice." Nathan took a drag on the bottle of Peach Snapple.

"It's a pack-rat's heaven," Zeke corrected him.

"Yeah." Nathan smiled wanly. "Sorry. My OCD is getting the better of me. I thought I had it under control, but the dog attack, and being in a place like this... Stress is a big trigger for me."

"Oh man. I'm sorry." A light went on in Zeke's head. "That's why you wanted the Xanax." He glanced outside. It was getting dark. "I can run to town right now—"

"It's all right. I can cope until tomorrow. The Xanax just helps take the edge off for a few hours; gives me time to cope. I've learned other ways to manage it."

"So... OCD. Like that TV detective, Monk?"

Nathan winced. "Yeah. Kinda. It's more complicated than that."

"How long have you had it?" Zeke's gaze lingered on Nathan's naked chest. He was feeling warmer than he ought to.

"Since I was ten." Nathan looked at the piles of stuff around the room.

Poor guy looked nervous as hell. "You think hoarding is a kind of OCD?" Zeke joked to lighten the mood.

Nathan snorted. "This isn't hoarding. It's survival."

"Yeah, I suppose you're right." Nathan was handsome, even

dirty as he was. Zeke decided that he wanted to kiss him rather badly.

He shifted his trousers. He wasn't usually so out of control like this.

Of course, Nathan had the whole *only other living human being on the face of the Earth* thing going for him. "So why didn't you drive?"

"Across country?"

"Sure. There must be plenty of cars still out there and enough gas for a thousand lifetimes."

"Probably so. But the roads are all filled with them too—wrecks and stalls and abandoned hulks. The freeways and streets near the cities and towns are all but impassable."

Zeke nodded. "Makes sense."

"Besides, I thought, 'what's the hurry?' There's no one waiting for me in Vancouver. I just want to get back there. It was my home." He snorted. "Stupid, huh?"

"Not really. I've been going through the motions here for a year." He took another bite of the trout. "I have a shortwave radio, but I haven't heard from anyone else in more than a year. I locked myself down at home with my rifle and enough ammunition to bring down an army. Eventually everything went silent. Quiet. Like when the world was first made."

"So what happened?"

"What do you mean?" The trout was salty, so he washed it down with a swig of beer.

"It was over so quickly in Vermont. By the time I woke up, everyone else was dead." Nathan put a hand on his knee to still his bouncing leg.

Zeke couldn't look away from Nathan's face. He shook his head, trying to dispel his romantic fantasies. "There were rumors on the shortwave that it was a terror attack; that the disease spread too readily to be natural; that it appeared in fifty places at once. Real news was hard to come by." That had been the blackest time of his life, knowing that people down in town were dying—friends and acquaintances—and there wasn't shit-all he could do about it.

Nathan looked out the window. "I remember getting sick and then going crazy, wanting to fuck anyone and everyone; not being able to stop. It was like OCD but a hundred times worse. I had no control over my own body. I was at this gay campground, and a hundred guys literally fucked themselves to death in front of me."

"You were sick?" What if Nathan was a carrier?

"I guess so. When I woke up, everyone else was dead."

Zeke thought about it. If Nathan had been a carrier, Zeke would already have been symptomatic. The plague was that fast. What good would it do to be afraid?

Besides, Nathan might be the only other guy left on the planet. Wasn't it worth it to take a chance?

Impulsively he set down his plate, leaned forward, and kissed Nathan on the lips.

Nathan didn't respond at first. Then he pushed Zeke away gently. "Sorry. I wasn't expecting that." He blushed again.

Zeke's face was on fire. *I'm an idiot.* "Hey, listen, I'm feeling a bit antsy. I think I'm gonna run down to town and get that Xanax for you tonight after all."

Nathan frowned. "It's okay. I can wait. Look, I didn't mean to—"

"Not a problem." It was clear that Nathan didn't see him *that way.*

"Um, okay?" He stared at Zeke for a moment, his face unreadable. "It's also called Alprazolam."

Zeke scrambled for the bobsled keys on the little table by the door. "Make yourself at home. I'll be back in a little while." He slipped out the door into the cool evening air and closed it behind him, leaning back against the thick wood and closing his eyes. *What the fuck is wrong with me?* He needed some space.

He hopped on the snowmobile and headed back into town.

NATHAN WATCHED the door slam closed.

His lips still tingled. Zeke had *kissed* him.

Which would have been welcome if he hadn't in the middle of a full-blown OCD episode. At least he'd have the meds soon enough. They might help forestall his compulsion storm.

At least that answered one question.

Nathan managed to get up slowly, collecting the dirty plates, and hobbled in the direction of the kitchen. He reached the doorway and stopped, shocked.

The place was an absolute mess.

The sink was filled with dirty dishes, and every surface was covered with junk: plates and pots and pans and small appliances in dangerous piles.

It's not safe.

He *had* to do something about it. That was the whole *compulsive* part of his disorder.

He sighed and gave in. It felt good, scratching that itch at last.

He set his own plate down and started in on the dirty dishes with a bucket of clean water he found on the counter, cleaning them one at a time and setting them on the floor. There were too many to lay singly. He thought he could deal with short stacks, maybe two or three high.

"What are you doing?"

Nathan turned to find Andy standing there, his arms crossed over his chest, leaning against the door frame. "Where the hell have *you* been?"

Andy shrugged. "I thought it was better if you met this guy alone. Now come on, put that plate down."

"I can't. I *have* to clean these up."

Andy frowned. "You don't have to do this, Nathan."

"It's not safe."

"You can get past this. You've done it before. Look, these dishes have been here for how long?"

Nathan stopped his scrubbing just long enough to look around. "Weeks? Months?"

"And did anything bad happen?"

"I don't know. I wasn't here." He washed another dish using the soap and a bottle of water by the sink.

"That's right. You weren't. Zeke is still alive. What if you hadn't come along?"

How the hell did Andy know Zeke's name? "I don't know."

Andy kept pushing. "Isn't it likely he would have been just fine?"

"Maybe. But..."

"... It's not safe. You already told me that."

Nathan nodded miserably.

"Listen, you know that's just the broken part of your brain talking, right?"

Nathan did know it, but he still *needed* to scratch that itch. It was *bad* this time, as bad as it had been since *before*.

What if he did *nothing*, and something happened to Zeke? How would he feel then?

Andy came to stand next to him. "What did Dr. Kapoor tell you?"

Nathan closed his eyes. "To face my fear. To see if something bad really does happen. But I can't..."

"Can't or won't?" Andy stared at him, his brown eyes boring into Nathan's.

"Why did you leave me alone?" Nathan could push back when he needed to. "You left me all alone when those dogs attacked, and then again on Zeke's porch." Maybe Andy didn't like him anymore.

"I never left you."

Nathan spat at him. "Fucking liar." He turned his back on his friend and resumed his scrubbing.

"Suit yourself."

Nathan was going through water quickly. He'd have to go find more or melt some snow.

When he looked back, Andy was gone.

AFTER HIS DISASTROUS flirtation with Nathan, Zeke decided it was best to sleep in town for the night. *He said he'd be okay for the night.*

Zeke had made himself a home away from home the year before, in a second-floor apartment over a coffee shop. It was perfect for when he wanted to do more advanced scavenging without having to return to the cabin. It was handy now too, when he needed to be alone. Still, he felt like an ass for leaving Nathan to his own devices.

He'd made a big fool of himself, and he needed some time to figure things out. He hadn't ever planned on seeing a living human being again, let alone one he was attracted to. It was as if fate had responded to his loneliness. And then to be rebuffed...

The universe really did hate his guts.

In any case, there was plenty for Nathan to eat in the cabin, and a night alone wouldn't kill him.

Zeke sat on the twin bed in the little apartment, his knees pulled up to his chest, wondering what was so wrong with him. The place was a bit musty, but he'd opened the window just a crack, and the cool air brought the smell of pine trees and snow with it.

After a while staring at the wall, his mind turned to other questions.

How had Nathan survived the plague? Other than himself, it had been one hundred percent fatal as far as he could tell. Then again, in a world of six billion people, there had to be a few who were immune, right? Or at least, who were able to fight it off?

In the end, the virus had been in the air and the water—just about everywhere, if the final reports were to be believed. *I must have been exposed at some point. If I was gonna get sick, it would have happened a long time ago.* Especially in the weeks immediately after the collapse.

Maybe I'm immune. He'd considered it before.

He'd go back to talk with Nathan in the morning. If Nathan didn't want to be his... boyfriend? Lover? Maybe Zeke could settle for being just friends.

It was far better than being alone.

THE DISHES WERE ALL CLEAN, arrayed around the kitchen in neat, short piles.

Nathan sat with his back against the kitchen cabinets, breathing hard. His leg wound had broken open again sometime during the frenzied cleaning, and blood trickled down his leg onto the floor.

He was exhausted.

It's not safe.

The little repeating thought in his head still poked at him. He no longer had the energy to do what it wanted.

He sighed and closed his eyes.

3

———————

December 21

Zeke woke up the next morning in his hideaway, feeling better about the state of the world. Surely Nathan was just feeling stressed. He'd said as much himself. *Maybe I didn't ruin everything.*

And even if he had, having someone else around, even as a friend, was far better than nothing.

He got dressed and tromped down the stairs from the apartment, looking around the little abandoned coffee shop. He still half expected Maribel to come through the double doors to the kitchen. *"You want some fries with that, hon?"*

So many ghosts. Time to move on.

Zeke walked down to Doug's Drug and pulled out a flashlight to search the pharmacy for Xanax. He couldn't remember if the drug was over the counter or prescription. He searched the shelves in front with no luck, and there was no one to ask.

He finally found it stored in the back of the pharmacy. They had five bottles, so he grabbed them all, along with a surprise for Nathan. *Call it a peace offering.*

He carried his haul back to the snowmobile, stepping out into the bright new day. The sun was shining, and the snow on the pavement was already melting into slush. He grimaced. At least the demise of humanity had probably slowed down the whole *global warming* thing.

He climbed onto the snowmobile and rode out of the ghost town.

Fifteen minutes later, he pulled up in front of the cabin and parked the snowmobile. He grabbed his bag of supplies from the back and rushed inside. He hoped Nathan had been comfortable enough in his absence. "Hey, Nathan, I'm back. Sorry, I got waylaid in town last night..."

The living room was empty. He set down the bag on the couch and looked around. "Nathan?"

It was cold inside. The fire had gone out.

He looked through the cabin, checking the two bedrooms first, then the bathroom, and finally the kitchen. "Oh God." Nathan lay sprawled on the tile floor, his leg bleeding again. He was surrounded by little stacks of clean dishes.

Zeke knelt and checked Nathan's pulse. It was weak but still there.

Shit. I'm an asshole. While he'd been tucked snugly away in his little hideaway in town, worried about that kiss, Nathan had been laying here all alone, maybe bleeding out.

Zeke touched Nathan's cheek gently. *I'm sorry.* Then he picked up Nathan gently to carry him to the guest room bed that he'd made up the day before. Nathan wasn't going to let the man slip away from him—not if he could help it.

He laid Nathan on top of the bed and put a towel under his leg. He unwrapped the biggest wound again. It looked bad. The skin around the puncture was red and angry-looking, dark lines ran up and down Nathan's leg—a clear sign of infection—and the wound itself wasn't healing properly. The antibiotics weren't working.

He ran to the bathroom and rummaged around in his medicine cabinet and found a bottle of erythromycin he'd taken when he'd cut his hand open pretty badly a couple years before. It was a month past the expiration date, but it was the only other antibiotic he had on hand.

He'd try that first. He could always run back to town for something else if it didn't help arrest the spread of the infection.

Zeke wrapped a new bandage around Nathan's leg to staunch the bleeding, then relit the fire to heat the place up. When the flames were going, he put some water in the kettle to boil.

He brought Nathan a glass of water, some Tylenol, a couple Xanax and some of the erythromycin. He propped up Nathan's head, and the man woke just enough to gulp down the pills. Zeke laid him back down gently, and he dropped back off to a deep slumber.

After the water had boiled, Zeke let it cool and used it with some soap to cleanse the wound once again. Nathan moaned when the cool water touched his skin, but he didn't wake again. The skin around it was red and warm to the touch.

Once it was clean, Zeke bandaged it up again and stepped back to look at his handiwork.

Nathan looked so small and vulnerable. Zeke just wanted to climb into bed and hold him, to tell him everything was going to be okay.

Instead, he washed himself up and then pulled down his copy of *The Fellowship of the Ring*. A valiant quest against a great evil—it seemed appropriate.

He sat in the chair next to his bed and began to read aloud.

"Three Rings for the Elven-kings under the sky..."

NATHAN SLIPPED THROUGH HIS DREAMS, tumbling from one world to the next, each one a plunge into cold water.

He relived the day when he'd first been diagnosed with OCD, after a strep virus had gone to his brain, and how his parents had insisted there was nothing wrong with him while his mind screamed otherwise.

He dreamed about Mr. Sanders, his first therapist, who had shown him how to move past his OCD, a process that had taken years.

And he dreamed about Adrian, his first high school boyfriend, who had been everything Nathan was not: strong, self-assured, beautiful.

Then the dog attack—growls and gnashing of teeth—and the sudden sharp pain in his arm and leg. He screamed, looking around wildly for Andy.

Then it started all over again.

The day he'd first been diagnosed.

His parents insisting that everything was fine.

Mr. Sanders. Adrian. Dog Bite.

And again.

ZEKE WATCHED Nathan with growing concern. The man was tossing and turning on the bed. He had thrown back the covers and was whispering urgently under his breath.

Zeke sat on the bed, putting a hand on Nathan's forehead. It was hot.

He went to find a clean washcloth, dipped it in some cool water and then sat next to Nathan on the bed and dabbed his forehead.

"It's gonna be all right," he whispered. He hoped to God it was true.

A SECOND STORM blew in from the north late in the morning, stronger than the one that had preceded it, howling up the valley with a vengeance. *I miss weather forecasts.*

Zeke fired up the shortwave radio, using up a little more gas from the generator. This time he spent nearly an hour searching the bands to no avail. After finding out he wasn't alone, he'd been so hopeful that he'd finally hear from someone else.

Finally, he flicked the power switch off and went outside in the blowing snow to turn off the generator. One of these days he'd have to steal one of his neighbor's solar systems… if he could figure out how to get it to work.

He hurried back inside, wrapping himself in a warm blanket. As the wind and snow continued to pound the cabin, Zeke sat next to the guest bed, reading to Nathan.

When the hobbits and Strider finally reached Weathertop, Zeke put the book down and looked at his charge.

Nathan was strong and good-looking. He'd been walking every day for the better part of a year and a half, after all. His long black hair wasn't tangled, not like Zeke's had been—he took good care of himself. He was sleeping soundly, and some of the color had returned to his face, filling out his sharp features.

His hands were red and swollen—he must have been cleaning and organizing the kitchen until he fell over from pure exhaustion.

Stupid, stupid, stupid. Why did I let this happen? Why had he stayed away?

He sat on the bed next to Nathan and pulled back the covers.

He stifled his sharp intake of breath—Nathan's leg looked much worse.

Zeke peeled back the bandage. The line of infection had spread up his thigh to his groin, and the area around the puncture wound was now an angry blotch of red, purple, and green.

Fucking hell. The antibiotics weren't helping at all.

Zeke went back to the bathroom, checking through his medicine cabinet again. He didn't have anything else.

Infections like this had been no big deal back in the old world. He could have called his doctor, or he could have checked the web for the best drug to treat a dog bite. Or even just have driven Nathan to the clinic in town.

Now, without appropriate intervention, Nathan could very well die from a stupid infection.

He had to go back into to town.

Zeke peered out the window. It had to be early afternoon, but it looked like it was eight o'clock at night out there. He looked back in on Nathan, and confirmed his fears. There was nothing for it. He *had* to go.

He scribbled out a quick note and left it on the nightstand. Then he got dressed in his thermal underwear, adding a pair of jeans on top of that and his father's bright-red ski suit, gloves, and ski goggles.

He grabbed a backpack and threw a few power bars he'd been saving inside just in case, along with his pup tent and a little propane stove. He hoped not to need them, but you never knew.

Then he went out into the blizzard.

The snowmobile was covered under a foot of snow. He dug it out with gloved hands and climbed onto it, starting it and gunning the engine. With a kick, it took off across the new-fallen snow, sending up a spray of snowflakes as he veered toward town.

He knew this route like he knew the back of his hand. He

followed the old dirt road his father had cleared from the highway up to the cabin, taking it slowly so he wouldn't miss a turn. Luckily the two storms hadn't yet managed to bury the old barbwire fence that bounded the south side of the road, so it provided a guide for him about halfway down the mountain.

From there it was a matter of following the stream bank.

Despite the warm clothing, Zeke was shivering, his beard covered in little icicles. The snow was letting up a little, and as he rounded a curve, Thompson Falls seemed to suddenly materialize in the river valley below. It looked like a Currier and Ives Christmas card, snow making all the roofs white. But there were no lights, and nothing living moving down there. *More like a Tim Burton Christmas.*

In another ten minutes, he reached Doug's again. He left the snowmobile running and pulled the door open, shining his flashlight through the gloom.

The pharmacy had to have a book on medications. Sure, it would have been all online, but this was Thompson Falls. Small-town pharmacy like this and all...

He found it in the back office. There, on a small bookshelf shoved up against a wall between two dead ficus plants, was a copy of the Physician's Desk Reference.

He pushed aside the junk littering the desk—old magazines, a laptop, and an empty bottle of Pepsi—and flipped the book open. "Antibiotics... antibiotics..." He found them in the index and began going through them one by one.

Then his flashlight flickered out.

"Fucking hell." He took the book with him, felt his way out to the public part of the pharmacy, and found a couple D cells to replace his dead ones. Then he resumed his search.

"Actinomycin... no. Aculeacin... no. Adenine... no.

Amoxicillin... aha!" The broad-spectrum antibiotic was recommended for treating puncture wounds.

He ran back into the dispensary and worked his way through the shelves. He found the spot labeled Amoxicillin. It was empty.

"Shit." *Think, Zeke, think.* When he'd come down here earlier for the Xanax, Nathan had mentioned its generic name. So if Amoxicillin was the generic name... he ran back to the counter and looked through the PDR again.

There it was. Amoxicillin was also sold under the brand names Moxatag and DisperMox.

Another search through the dispensary turned up a small bin of Moxatag. "Bingo!" He grabbed all of them and threw them into an empty bottle, shoving it into his jacket pocket. *Time to get back to Nathan.*

Climbing onto the snowmobile, he spun around and took off toward the cabin.

The snowfall had started up again, and the wind was kicking up, throwing it into his face.

In his hurry, he missed the turnoff for the road that led up to the cabin and lost fifteen minutes circling back to find it.

He was about a third of the way home, by his best reckoning, when he realized he wasn't going to make it. The snowfall was so heavy it was blinding him, and if he wasn't careful, he'd drive himself into a ditch, dooming both himself and Nathan.

He'd have to wait out the storm.

Reluctantly, he pulled off the road and veered toward the rising canyon walls. He found a semi-sheltered spot next to a rock overhang, cleared out the snow, and set up his little tent. Then he packed a wall of snow next to it to act as insulation.

He climbed inside, shivering violently, and lit the propane stove, making sure there was room for airflow so he wouldn't die of carbon monoxide poisoning. Then he sat with his back against the rock, through the tent fabric, and munched on one of his energy bars while the wind howled outside.

Over the last year, Zeke's days had fallen into a predictable routine. Wake, eat, forage, eat, sleep.

Now though, there was an unexpected new variable, and he wasn't sure how things were going to change. Even if Nathan didn't like him *that way*, at least he'd have someone to talk to.

Things were exciting, but suddenly he found himself longing for normal again. His own warm bed back home, for starters.

One thing he was sure of. His old routines were gone for good.

~

NATHAN TOSSED AND TURNED, caught in the throes of a nightmare, only half aware that none of it was real.

His mind dragged him back through those three days of hell in the cabin in Vermont, when he'd been overtaken by the plague. When he'd been reduced from the man he knew himself to be to little more than a crazed, lust-filled animal.

He relived the nights of terror he'd experienced as a child, when he'd first been afflicted with his OCD.

It's not safe!

Finally, he woke in a cold sweat. His leg ached and throbbed. He pulled the covers back weakly. It was infected, and looked like crap. That much he could tell in the dim light. "Zeke," he croaked, his throat dry. "Zeke!"

But Zeke didn't answer.

He was sweating. The sheets were soaked. But he was too tired to get up to do anything about it.

Instead, he plunged once more into a troubled sleep.

4

December 22

Zeke woke, wincing at the cramp in his left leg. The storm had blown itself out, and it looked to be morning outside.

The rock face was hard and uneven against his back through the fabric of the tent. The space inside was surprisingly comfortable, though he'd run out of propane some time before.

He stretched as much as he was able in the small tent and rubbed his cramped leg. Once he felt like he could move again, he pushed his way outside to gaze at the layer of new-fallen snow. The sun was out, and the light sparkled off the white snowbanks like a thousand fireflies.

He sucked in his breath. It was beautiful.

Nathan was waiting for him though, and the storm had delayed him. His infection would be getting worse by the hour.

Zeke dug out the snowmobile frantically, sending snow flying in all directions. He could come back for the tent later. At last he had it free, and he climbed on it to start the engine. He checked his pockets and stopped dead in his tracks.

The bottle of Moxatag was gone.

"No, no, no, no, no, no, no..."

He scrambled back inside the tent, checking each of the corners. It wasn't there.

"Looking for this?"

A man was standing a few feet from the snowmobile. He was average looking—maybe six feet tall, mousy brown hair, brown eyes. He was pointing at the ground.

The bottle lay there, cupped by the snow. It must have fallen out of his pocket while he was digging out the snowmobile.

"Who are you?" How had this man found him, out in the middle of nowhere?

"Take them back to him. He needs you." He winked and faded away into nothing.

Zeke blinked. It couldn't be. "Andy?" He looked around, but he was all alone in the hollow. There was no answer. He rubbed his eyes—maybe he was tired. *I'm hallucinating.*

He reached down to pick up the bottle. It was real enough.

He looked around for some sign that the man had been real, but there was nothing, not even footprints. With a sigh, he mounted the snowmobile and set off toward the cabin.

He made it in ten minutes, jumping off the vehicle to bound up onto the porch. He ran inside and grabbed a bottled water.

Nathan was asleep on the bed. His forehead was hot, and he was still agitated, tossing and turning. Zeke managed to get him into a sitting position and got some of the Moxatag down his throat, along with some Xanax and Tylenol.

He changed the bandages again, frowning at how much farther the infection had spread in such a short time.

He left his charge to rest and got the fire going again, warming the cabin and casting a cheery glow across the living room.

Then he settled in to read a bit more of Tolkien's masterwork to Nathan.

All he could do now was to repeat the dosage every six hours and wait.

5

———————

December 23

Nathan recognized the warm, fuzzy glow around his consciousness. *Xanax.* Zeke must have found some and dosed him up.

The room was dimly lit by the dim glow coming in through the one window, framed by heavy red drapes. The wind was howling outside, but it was warm in the cabin. From the light, he guessed that it was probably late afternoon or early evening.

Zeke was asleep in an armchair next to the bed.

Nathan watched him for a few moments. Asleep, he looked ten years younger, the lines of his face smoothed out. He tried to imagine Zeke as a teenager—he might have looked a little like Adrian. Nathan smiled at the thought. *I miss you, Addie.*

He pulled back the sheet to see the damage. His leg still looked *bad*, but it didn't hurt as much. He pushed himself up, wincing as the movement strained his leg wounds. "Ouch."

Zeke stirred, looking up at him and smiling. Despite the man's butchered haircut, he *was* attractive, with a ruggedly handsome face. "Morning."

Nathan laughed. "More like evening. How long was I out?"

"Three days." Zeke sat up and grimaced, rubbing his back. "I found you on the kitchen floor. You've been sleeping ever since—I think the infection took a lot out of you." He glanced at Nathan's leg. "It looks better."

"It feels better." He stretched the leg just a little, and pain lanced his wound. "Owww."

"Look, I'm so sorry I left you alone—"

"I get it. You freaked out."

"Yeah. Something like that." Zeke looked uncomfortable. "I can be a real idiot sometimes."

Nathan closed his eyes. *You're not the only one.* "Don't worry about it." He looked around, taking in the overflowing bookshelves and the gas lamp on the nightstand by the bed. "Hey, did Andy ever come back?"

"Nope. No one but you here, I'm afraid. Your friend must have deserted you." Zeke squirmed a little, rubbing his back again. "There were no footprints."

Andy was just a figment of his imagination. Nathan was sure of that now. The mind could do funny things to a guy, especially when he was alone for such a long time. Though why he hadn't realized it before...

He closed his eyes. *Of course. I am an idiot.* "Andy" had been there before, too, when he was little, only his name had been Andrew then. His imaginary friend. When his OCD had started, Andrew had helped him through it.

It had been so long ago, he'd all but forgotten it. Andy had been younger then, too, and shy. Shyer than Nathan.

His wandering mind had conjured up his old "friend" again when he'd been needed the most.

They sat in silence for a few moments, each lost in his thoughts. The wind blustered outside, and the flickering of the lamp sent shadows scudding across the ceiling like dark clouds.

At last, the pressure in Nathan's bladder forced the issue. "I think I need to take a piss." He blushed. "Would you help me to the bathroom?" He hated being so dependent on someone else, let alone a stranger.

"Sure. Come on." Zeke put an arm under Nathan's and carefully helped him out of bed. Zeke was a good three inches shorter than Nathan's six-foot-one.

Together they made their way to the toilet, banging into the wall painfully more than once. Zeke's arm was warm under his.

His host maneuvered him down onto the toilet seat and handed Nathan a towel to cover his naked body.

In a moment, Nathan's bladder released into the water in the toilet basin. "Oh my God, that feels good." He looked at the toilet tank. "How do you keep it working?"

"Gravity and stream water," Zeke said, kicking the five-gallon bucket next to the bowl. "These old gravity-feed tanks don't need anything else, and the septic tank was emptied a month before the plague. So it's good for another three-to-five years."

Nathan flushed the toilet, and Zeke refilled it from the bucket. "Voila." He sniffed Nathan. "I know I'm no prize, but you're pretty ripe. You up for a bath?"

Nathan stared at the bathtub, doubtful. "How are you going to pull that off?"

"Snowmelt plus some water heated over the fire."

Nathan nodded. "Oh my God, I'd love a hot bath." He caught Zeke looking over his mostly naked body and smiled. "Can I ask you something?" he said, though he was pretty sure he already knew the answer.

Zeke nodded. "Anything."

"You're gay, right?"

Zeke blushed. "I'm... yes. I am." He sighed. "I've never actually told anyone before."

"Seriously?" Nathan asked. The man had to be in his mid-forties, at least. "It's the twenty-first Century, even here in Montana"

Zeke held up two fingers. "Scout's honor."

Nathan laughed, delighted. "Well, doesn't that beat all?"

"What's that?"

"The last, best hope for humanity is a couple gay guys."

"A couple...?" Zeke stared at him for a moment, then burst out laughing. "Adam and Eve have nothing on us."

Nathan had missed real human contact. Intimacy and speech, sure, but especially touch. "I'd like it very much if you'd help me take a bath."

Zeke blushed again. "Stay right there. I'll get the water ready." Then he bustled out of the room, leaving a bemused but aroused Nathan to stare after him in wonder.

ZEKE POURED the hot water from the kettle into the lukewarm water already in the bucket and carried it back into the bathroom. "Let's get you in the tub," he said, holding out an arm to support the still-weak Nathan. He unwrapped the towel from Nathan's waist, and noticed that Nathan seemed *interested* in him, too. Maybe he'd misread the signals before.

Zeke helped him negotiate the white porcelain ledge of the bathtub. They got him seated inside, slowly and carefully, and placed the towel over him again. "I don't think I've been washed by someone else since I was a kid." Nathan was smiling.

"I did this a lot for my mother, toward the end. She had cancer, and she got to the point where she couldn't take care of herself anymore."

Nathan nodded. "Good to know I'm in expert hands."

"Something like that." He looked at Nathan's hair. "Why don't we start with this? Do you want it cut or just washed?"

"A wash is fine." He smirked. "There weren't many salons on the way here."

Zeke chuckled. He used a bowl to pour some warm water over Nathan's head, tilting it back so it ran away from Nathan's eyes. Then he took some shampoo and massaged it deep into Nathan's scalp.

"Oh my God, that feels good," Nathan said, closing his eyes. "I forgot what getting clean felt like. What... what someone else's touch felt like."

Zeke chuckled. For his part, Zeke was enjoying the contact too. "I have a confession to make."

Nathan opened one eye and looked up at him through the streaming suds. "You already told me you're gay."

"Yeah, this is... well... the day you showed up here, I had kinda let myself go, personal hygiene-wise. I mean, no one to care, right?"

"You look all right to me."

Zeke snorted. "Yeah, here's the thing about that. After I made sure your wounds were cleaned up and you were all in one piece, I might have cleaned myself up a bit." *If I'd known you were coming...*

Nathan laughed, a rich hearty sound. "I don't think we can hold ourselves—or each other—to the old standards anymore. We may well be the only survivors—that means we get to make our own rules."

"Maybe so. Close your eyes." He rinsed the shampoo out of Nathan's hair, letting it run down to the drain. The water came out soapy and dirty. "Let me shampoo you one more time. I think you had things living in there."

Nathan laughed. "Like you're one to talk."

"Fair." Zeke shifted, rearranging his jeans. He got another palmful of shampoo, lathered up Nathan's hair, and then rinsed it out again. This time the water came out clean.

Zeke stepped back to take a look. "Better. It won't get you a modeling job, but it looks good enough."

"Yeah, I don't think there are any modeling agencies left, this side of hell. God, how I hated those perfect guys in the magazines with their washboard abs and hairless airbrushed chests."

"And blindingly white teeth." He looked over Nathan's naked body. "Still, you're good-looking enough for it." Zeke blushed as he realized what he'd just said.

Nathan just smiled.

Zeke retrieved a fresh bar of soap and a clean washcloth from under the sink, dipping the cloth into the bucket and soaping it up. "OK, let's get the rest of you cleaned up."

"I... think I'm strong enough to do that myself."

Zeke tried not to notice the bulge under the towel over Nathan's waist. He suppressed a grin. "Um... sure. Here you go." He pulled the bucket over to where it was easy to reach and gave Nathan the soap and towel. "I'll be in the living room. Just holler when you're ready to rinse off."

He stepped outside and closed the door, leaning against the wall of the hallway with his eyes closed. A rush of contradictory emotions filled him: arousal, excitement, and shame.

Still the shame.

His father had caught him with Tom Higgins out in the woods once when he was seventeen and had literally dragged Zeke to the woodshed for a beating. He could still see the look of disgust and disappointment on his father's face. "There are no faggots in *my* family," he'd snarled.

They'd never spoken of it again.

His father was long dead now, and he'd never found the courage to come out to the man. So was the rest of the town, for that matter. Literally every other person who might have cared was gone. *So why am I still ashamed?*

It felt *so good* to be clean. Nathan shivered as the cool air touched his wet skin.

He stood in the tub, holding onto the metal support rail Zeke had probably put in for his mother as his host poured the rest of the water over his body, washing away the soap and dirt. He still couldn't believe his luck, to have run across someone else in this wide world who was still alive—and gay to boot—but he wanted to take it slow. *If I screw this up...* There weren't any more fish in the sea.

Fortunately his hard-on had subsided. His mind was still a little wooly from the Xanax, and the short bath had exhausted his limited resources. He was ready for bed.

Zeke helped him dry off.

"Thank you," Nathan said as Zeke supported him on the way back to the bedroom. "I feel badly taking your bed." He fought to stay awake.

"Mine's upstairs, but I would have given it to you willingly." Zeke's eyes twinkled. "Besides, that mattress is lumpy as hell." Zeke eased him down onto the edge of the bed. "Let me bandage you up again before you lie down." He knelt to check the bites, and Nathan, even in his worn-out state, was keenly aware of Zeke's proximity to his crotch. With just a nudge of his hand, he could have...

He sighed. He was far too tired to enjoy it anyway.

"It's looking much better. The new antibiotics seem to be

working." Zeke took some new bandages from the nightstand and lifted Nathan's leg gently to wrap them around the wound.

"New antibiotics?"

"Yes, I had to run back to town to get them. Got stuck out in the storm overnight too." He finished the wrap. "There. Let's get you back in bed."

The window rattled. "Big storm outside?"

Zeke nodded. "Third one this week. It'll blow itself out in another day or so. You made it here just in time."

"I know." Nathan accepted another handful of drugs and then felt the covers and heavy blanket being pulled over his naked body. They were cool at first, but he warmed up quickly, his body wrapped in linens and his mind in a soft cloud of drugs. "Zeke?" he whispered as he settled into sleep.

"What?"

He stared up into Zeke's kind eyes. Everything was warm and wonderful. "Thank you." He felt sleep rising up to envelop him. "I think I love you."

I THINK *I* LOVE YOU.

Zeke stood at his living room window, looking out at the swirling snow. The latest storm had dumped about a foot and a half of snow so far, covering everything in white, but the clouds painted the landscape a morose gray.

He *knew* Nathan hadn't meant it, at least not in a romantic sense. The man was exhausted and drugged, and he was so pumped full of drugs that he had to be feeling pretty damned good right about now.

And yet...

No man had ever said that to him before. He tried to imagine it, for real, what it would be like to be *loved* by another man. By Nathan.

His father's picture stared at him from its frame on the mantel. The man's eyes were hard, cold, his face captured in an eternal frown.

Zeke closed his eyes and heard his father's voice again. "*Faggot.*" He growled and opened them again, glaring at the man who had made him feel this way about himself.

He was done with being ashamed.

He grabbed the frame and slipped open the back, pulling out the photograph. "I'm done with you, you fucking jerk," He crumpled up the photo and threw it into the fireplace. It burst into flame, giving off a blue glow and a strong chemical smell.

His father hadn't been a good man. He wasn't just *rough*. He'd been a homophobic, backwoods asshole. *I'm done with you. At last.*

A great weight lifted off Zeke's shoulders, and he felt better than he had in years.

Outside, the hills darkened.

Inside, Zeke threw another log on the fire, rekindling the flame that had almost gone out.

6

December 24

Zeke woke up feeling refreshed. He'd slept soundly, even though he'd been on the old couch and not in his own bed upstairs.

He popped into the bedroom to check on Nathan. The man was snoring away, oblivious as yet to the new morning. Zeke realized he finally had his wish. He was no longer alone.

The storm had passed during the night, and the sun was just coming up over the mountaintops, its bright rays blinding over the fresh snow. He looked out into his front yard, into a world sparkling with possibility.

Zeke crept out of the room, careful not to wake Nathan, and into the kitchen. He'd put away the dishes Nathan had washed, but he still wasn't used to it being so clean and organized. It was quite a change, keeping everything in its place, though his mother had been exceptionally good at maintaining the cabin in exquisite order.

His usual shortwave exercise turned up nothing new—why he still hoped it would, after all this time, was beyond him.

His newfound enthusiasm for the task was starting to dim.

He grabbed his permanent marker and went into the garage to cross off the previous date. Then he stared at the calendar.

Tomorrow was Christmas Day. Holidays like Christmas and Thanksgiving and even his own birthday had ceased to matter when he was all alone, but now... If ever there had been a reason for him —for humankind—to celebrate Christmas, this was it.

Unless Nathan wasn't Christian... Were they Christian up in Canada? He snorted. *You're a a real idiot about some things, Zeke.*

It didn't matter. They *had* to celebrate.

He went out to the garage to check on the artificial tree he'd found at the store. He pulled it out of its bag and frowned. It was old and rusted and smelled of mold.

He could do better.

Whistling, he grabbed his axe, opened the garage door, and set out in search of the perfect Christmas tree.

Nathan awoke to an unbelievable sound.

Music. And not just any music.

Deck the halls with boughs of holly,
Fa la la la la la la la la.

He eased himself up in bed, looking around the dimly-lit room. His leg felt much better now, though it still ached when he stretched the skin. He looked at it. The dark lines were fading, and it didn't hurt so much to touch it.

. . .

'Tis the season to be jolly,
  Fa la la la la la la la la.

NATHAN GRINNED, anticipating the next line as he swung his legs carefully over the side of the bed. He winced as he put weight on his injured leg, but the pain was bearable.

Don we now our gay apparel,
  Fa la la la la la la la la.

HE LIMPED over to the closet to look for something to put on and found an old, worn bathrobe.

Join the ancient yuletide carol,
  Fa la la la la la la la la.

HE PADDED out barefoot to find Zeke in the living room, grinning at him like a fool.

There was an eight-foot tree by the fireplace, adorned with strings of garland and homemade ornaments, and there were sparkling Christmas lights too

It was like a scene out of his childhood.

"What's all this?"

Zeke laughed. "It's Christmas Eve today. Close as I can tell anyhow. Come take a seat."

Nathan sat on the couch, staring at the lights in wonder. "How did you..."

"Oh, those. Couple gallons of gas in the generator. It will run out in three or four hours, but I thought it was worth it for the occasion." He sat down next to Nathan. "Sorry, there's no eggnog. I *do* have a hundred-year-old bottle of Scotch." He held up a bottle filled with golden liquid.

"Better not. With the Xanax..." He allowed himself to be steered to the couch.

"Oh. Of course." Zeke blushed.

Nathan just stared at the tree. "It's... beautiful. I never thought I'd see another Christmas... or Christmas tree." He reached out to touch one of the branches. It was soft and fresh. "You did all of this?"

"I wanted this to be special." He looked like a scared puppy dog. "You like it?"

He nodded. "I love it." He looked at the bottle of Scotch again. "Maybe just a sip."

Zeke grinned. He poured them a couple fingers each. They sat down together on the couch and stared at the tree.

"It's fresh cut. It *smells* like Christmas."

Zeke nodded. "We always had an artificial tree. Mom was allergic to the real thing, or something. Maybe she just didn't like cutting down a living thing. But now..."

Nathan nodded. "It's nice to have a little normal. More than nice." His eyes were wet. He was filled with contradictory emotions. Happiness, regret, a deep sadness, and... love?

"It is, at that." Zeke held up his glass, and they clinked them together. "Cheers." Together they downed the Scotch.

It was awful. Nathan hacked and coughed up half of it all over his borrowed bathrobe. "I'm so sorry..." he said, feeling embarrassed. He was such a mess.

Zeke laughed. "Don't be. You were right. We have to learn not to be sorry anymore. Or ashamed." He pointed at the natty old robe. "Here, give that to me. I'll get you something else to wear."

Nathan stood unsteadily and shrugged his way out of the garment, aware that he was once again naked in front of Zeke.

Zeke took the robe, and they stood face to face for a minute.

Zeke had done all this for him. This and so much more. "Did I… tell you I loved you, yesterday?"

Zeke looked away. "You were on a lot of drugs."

"I think I meant it." *Caution be damned.* Nathan pulled Zeke gently into a kiss, feeling him tense up and then relax.

It lasted a long time, sending a long-forgotten warmth coursing through Nathan's body. He remembered Adrian's lips, softer than Zeke's, without the stubble. His first crush. *This is so much better.*

When they separated, Zeke's eyes were twinkling. "I was afraid you didn't like me, when I kissed you before."

Nathan shook his head. "I *liked* you just fine. But I was in the throes of a full OCD meltdown. I wasn't able to handle it just then."

"But now?"

Nathan nodded. "Now."

Zeke was shaking. He pulled off his shirt, revealing a thick, hairy chest. Then he shrugged out of his jeans and white briefs, though they might have been a little gray, revealing… a lot more.

Nathan grinned. He put his hand on Zeke's shoulder. "You don't have to be scared," he said softly.

"I'm not." Zeke kissed him again, and then pulled him gently down onto the new rug by the fireplace. He kissed Nathan's lips, then his neck, eliciting a groan.

Nathan got hard. It had been too long. He put his arms around Zeke, digging his fingers into the hard muscles of Zeke's back.

Zeke worked his way down, playing with Nathan's nipples and sending him into heaven.

Zeke dropped his hands to the floor, squeezing the fibers of the rug between his fingers, arching his back as he rose on the waves of his building pleasure. "Oh fuuuuck," he growled, and it didn't take long for him reach climax, his mind spinning in all the best ways. He spasmed with pleasure, once, twice, three times, and then fell back onto the rug, spent in more ways than one.

"Merry Christmas," Zeke said with a wicked grin.

"I want to return the favor," Nathan said, reaching for Zeke.

"Later. When you're stronger. For now, I just want to be close to you." He lay down next to Nathan and wrapped an arm over his chest, snuggling into his neck.

They lay there for a long time, intertwined on the heavy rug. Eventually they fell asleep together in front of the crackling fire.

NATHAN WOKE, his heart racing, pounding his ribcage like that thing in *Alien*. It was amazing he didn't burst right open.

It was dark in the cabin, the glow of the embers providing the only light. Zeke was asleep next to him, turned away toward the fire.

The stacks of *things* loomed over him like misshapen monsters.

It's not safe.

The little voice was becoming more insistent. It wanted him to *make it safe*. To put everything around him in its place. To expend all his energy on a stupid and futile task.

He *knew* it was senseless.

Knowing it didn't lessen the compulsion.

He could take more Xanax. He was sure he could find the bottle in this little place, or he could wake Zeke and ask him for it.

But the Xanax wouldn't last forever. Sooner or later, he would run out again, or the pills would expire and slowly lose their effectiveness.

What would he do then?

Plus it dulled him *somehow*; made him feel less *Nathan*.

He closed his eyes. What if he didn't do anything? What if he left everything stacked in piles and on tables and chairs in the cabin exactly as it was? What would happen?

Nothing, he told the little broken part of his brain.

It's not safe.

The compulsion pulled at him.

It's not my fault. He knew, logically, what caused his compulsions. He'd learned to move past them before, without medication. His therapist had helped him with that, and it had worked for years.

If he'd done it before, he could do it again.

It's not safe.

He needed to be outside, away from the triggers all around him. He needed to short-circuit his brain.

Nathan stood quietly, not wanting to wake Zeke. He picked up the stained, tattered old robe, pulled it on, and forced himself to ignore the siren call of his broken mind. His body shook with anxiety as he moved past all the piles of things.

Zeke had left his own hiking boots by the entry. Nathan pulled them on without socks and quietly opened the front door, letting himself out onto the porch. Zeke must have shoveled off the snow that morning because the porch was clear.

It was cold as hell, or maybe heaven? But Zeke didn't mind. It shocked the little voice inside of him to silence.

He stepped down off the wooden porch and onto the fresh snow.

The night was lit by the waning moon, casting a silver glow

across the snow-covered landscape. The air was crisp but still. Nathan took a dozen steps into the yard and looked around.

It was breathtaking—like a scene right out of "Winter Wonderland."

"There's still beauty in the world, you know."

Nathan turned, half expecting Parson Brown.

Instead, it was Andy.

He knew he must look a mess, standing in the snow in a dirty bathrobe and hiking boots, unshaven and scruffy as shit. He didn't care. "Hello, Andy."

"You look good." Andy's nose twitched.

"Fucking liar. I don't even know why I'm talking to you." He peered at the man in the dim light. "You're not real, are you?"

Andy shrugged. "Define real."

"You're not human. A person. Flesh and blood, like me."

"Well, no. When you put it that way, I suppose I'm not." He held out his hand. "Why don't you come up on the porch and we can talk?"

Nathan stared at it suspiciously. Andy had *never* touched him before. What if he reached out, and there was nothing there but air?

What if I'm going crazy?

It's not safe.

"Fuck it." He reached out and grasped Andy's hand. It was as solid as his own. He stared at his old friend for a moment, and the shock must have been evident on his face.

"Toldja so." Andy grinned. He helped Nathan back onto the wooden porch, and they sat in the old metal swing rocker by the door.

For a long moment, they stared out at the snow together in silence.

A blessed peace settled over Nathan, one he hadn't known since before the plague days. Everything was calm. There were no demands on him, external or internal—even the little voice had gone silent, for once.

At last, he worked up the courage to ask the question that had been plaguing him for days. "What are you, then?"

"I don't know." Andy grimaced. "Not exactly."

Nathan snorted. It wasn't the answer he'd expected. "Well, that's satisfying."

Andy laughed. "Hey, I'm trying here. I'm... I guess you might call me your guardian angel."

"My what?" Nathan tried to sound indignant and full of disbelief, but he was too tired for it. He laughed instead. "I should have known. Hell of a job you've been doing." He rubbed his bandaged leg lightly. "Where were you when the dogs attacked me? When the plague hit? Damn, where were you when I got sick in the first place? My life would have been a hell of a lot better without this damaged brain."

Andy nodded. "I understand why you feel like that." He sighed, his gaze locked on the winter scene before him. "Believe me, I do. But it doesn't work that way. You wouldn't have been *you* without all those things."

"What do you mean?"

"A guardian angel isn't meant to keep you safe from every little thing in life, or even every big thing. Especially not the things you can handle yourself. Take the dogs, for instance."

"Yes, please do." Nathan grinned at his own joke.

Andy snorted, unimpressed. "You fought them off on your own. Being injured forced you to come face to face with your OCD again, and it let you be vulnerable in front of Zeke."

"I suppose..."

"And your OCD. It's a heavy burden, sure, but it changed you in other ways too. Made you more open to the struggles of others. More caring. A better human being."

Nathan blushed. "I would have been healthier, better."

"My point is that without those things, you wouldn't be *you*. I mean, look at you. You're gorgeous." He turned to stare at Nathan.

Nathan knew that *look*. "Um, thank you?" A gay guardian angel? *I've seen stranger things.* He considered it. He would have been healthier, and life would have sure been easier. But maybe Andy was right. He liked who he was when he wasn't in the thralls of his compulsions. "You mean I would have been a total dick?"

"Would have been?" Andy raised an eyebrow.

Nathan laughed ruefully. "Touché."

Nathan nodded. "Everybody has shit they have to deal with."

"That's true. Or it used to be." He stared at Andy for a moment. "I suppose the plague was all part of some grand plan?"

Andy shook his head. "That was all you. Humankind. You exercised your free will. More things. Better technology. More ways to kill each other, faster and more efficiently. The plague was just the last in a long, long line of death and destruction. And here we are."

Nathan took that in. It was a hell of a thing to process. "So what are you here for?" he asked at last.

"To pick up the pieces. To listen to you when you're all alone and to give you a nudge when you need it. How do you think you ended up *here*?" He gestured to the cabin.

Nathan thought about it. Andy had suggested coming this way, even though they chanced being trapped in these mountains in the winter.

He wondered how many other times he'd been subtly guided to or away from something without knowing it. "You were there when I was little too, weren't you?"

Andy nodded. "That's when I was first assigned to you. You were such a wonderful child. The compulsions might have killed you, but you were so strong."

"Thanks. I don't always feel strong."

"I know." He took Zeke's hand in his. His palm radiated heat, and Nathan realized he wasn't cold anymore. "You got past them once. You can do it again. You and Zeke still have a role to play in the future of things, you know."

Nathan snorted. "What future? Don't get me wrong. I'm thrilled to have found him. But what lies ahead? At best, maybe we get a few more good years living off the ruins. Then it's lights out. For everything. In case you forgot, we can't have kids."

Andy grinned. "What makes you think you two are the only ones?"

Nathan stared at him. "We aren't?"

"Wait until the winter is over and then head south. There are more of you—and more of us." Andy leaned forward and kissed him on the cheek. There was warmth there too, and something else.

Longing.

Then he grinned, and was gone, his smile lingering in the air half a second longer, Cheshire-cat style.

It's not safe.

The voice back, but it was thin and plaintive.

Nathan chose—this time—to ignore it.

He looked around at the porch and the cabin, and thought about Zeke inside.

He'd gotten his wish—he'd found his way home with a little help. Just not the home he'd expected.

As Christmas Eve ended and Christmas Day began, he went back inside and woke Zeke, leading him back to the guest room.

They snuggled in together under the warm blankets, and he snuggled next to Zeke's beautiful body, falling quickly to sleep.

7

December 25

Zeke slipped out of bed, careful not to wake Nathan. They'd slept together for the first time, actually slept—something Zeke had only dreamed of his entire life—and this morning he had awoken next to his... partner? Lover? Husband? They would define it later. He felt... *Optimistic*. That was the word.

He put some fresh logs on the fire, breathing in the fresh piney smell of the Christmas tree.

He headed into the bathroom, trimmed his beard again, and tried to even out his haircut, wanting to make it look its best with his limited barbering skills.

He brushed his teeth and put on a little deodorant. Soon he felt presentable enough.

He crept back into the bedroom and woke Nathan with a kiss. "Morning, sleepyhead."

Nathan stretched. "Morning." A lazy smile stretched across his face. "Merry Christmas."

He handed Nathan a package wrapped in paper towel and tied up with twist ties.

Nathan looked at it with a raised eyebrow.

"I didn't have time to run to town for wrapping paper. Open it!"

"I didn't get anything for you."

Zeke laughed, It felt good to laugh again. "You're my present this year."

Nathan snorted. He pulled off the makeshift paper and ribbon. "Oh my God, are you serious? Hershey's Special Dark?" He held up the candy bar.

"I found it in town."

"It's perfect." He pulled off the wrapper and the aluminum foil. He broke it down the middle and offered half to Zeke. "Where did you get it?"

Zeke smiled. "I remembered I hadn't quite cleaned out the chocolate supply at the drug store." He put his hand on Nathan's. "How are you?"

"The OCD, you mean?"

Zeke nodded.

"It's always going to be there. But today's OK. Better."

Zeke gave him a quick kiss. "I'm going to check the shortwave. Then I'll make us some breakfast. Man, I miss bacon and eggs."

"There must still be pigs and chickens somewhere."

Zeke grinned. "I suppose. Be back in a couple minutes." Zeke went into his library room and sat down at the shortwave radio. He worked his way through the bands for ten minutes. Nothing but static and more static.

He was just about to get up to make breakfast when he heard something.

He backed up the dial, and sure enough there it was.

Tap, tap, tap.

He sat back down in his seat and raised the volume to the max.

Nothing.

He reached to turn it off.

"Merry Christmas, world! This is Johnny Fever at WKRP, coming to you live from Cincinatti, spinning your Christmas tunes all day long. We'll start with an old favorite, "Winter Wonderland.""

Zeke stared at the shortwave, dumbfounded, as the first strains of the old Perry Como song played in his garage. *WKRP? Seriously?*

More importantly, there was someone else still alive out there?

He pressed the talk button on his microphone. "Um, hello?"

The music went dead.

"What's going on?" Nathan said, poking his head into the room. "I thought I heard music."

"Hello?" A voice said from the speaker simultaneously.

"Holy shit." Nathan came to stand next to Zeke. "Is that someone else?"

"I think so," Zeke whispered. "Hi, you're alive! I mean, I'm Zeke. Who is this?"

"Hey Zeke! This is Davis and Mari. Hot damn, it's good to hear another voice." The man's voice was deep and warm.

"Roger that," Zeke said. "Where are you?"

"Santa Fe, New Mexico. And you?"

"Up in Montana. Why have we never heard from you before?"

There was a short pause. "Mari just figured out how to hook up this shortwave radio we found to a generator. We figured we'd give the world a little Christmas joy."

Zeke realized he was tearing up. "Well, happy fucking Christmas."

Davis laughed. "Roger that."

Nathan sat down with Zeke, and together they talked with Davis and Mari for hours, comparing notes. The couple had been on an extended hiking trip out in the Carson National Forest and had returned home to find that the world had ended in their absence.

Zeke smiled up at Nathan frequently, squeezing his hand with excitement.

"You should come down here in the Spring," Davis said toward the end. "We have everything we need, plus it's a great place to grow things."

Zeke looked up at Nathan, who nodded. "We'd love that. As soon as the winter ends."

They signed off at last and agreed to talk again the next day.

Nathan stared at the shortwave, still stunned by the development. Andy had said, *Wait until the winter is over and then head south.*

Nathan turned back to Zeke and gave him a big hug. "I wished I could get home," he whispered. "And here I am."

"And I wished for someone to be with, and here you are." Zeke laughed.

"Merry Christmas," Nathan whispered into Zeke's ear. Things were going to be all right now—he was sure of it. Whatever came their way, they would deal wth it. Together.

Nathan went to the window. The sun was shining ouside, and the snow-covered hills were sparkling, nearly blinding him with the glare. Wonderland, indeed. Zeke came to stand next to him, and they looked out the scene together.

Somehow, he wasn't surprised to see Andy standing there, next to the cabin's old mailbox, staring at the sun.

Zeke's eyebrow raised. "Your friend?"

"You're not surprised?"

"He came to me too. In the snow, when I thought I'd lost your meds."

Nathan laughed. "Sounds like Andy."

"Is he…?"

"I'll tell you later." He slipped a hand around Zeke's waist.

As if sensing Nathan, his guardian angel turned and smiled, and raised his hand to wave.

Nathan grinned and waved back.

Then Andy turned to walk away, vanishing into the bright morning air.

ABOUT THE AUTHOR

I live with my husband of 28 years in a Sacramento, California suburb, in a little yellow house with a brick fireplace and a couple pink flamingoes.

As a writer, I've always lived between *here and now* and *what could be*. Indoctrinated into fantasy-sci fi by my mother at the tender age of nine, I devoured her library. But as I grew up and read the golden age classics and modern works, I began to wonder where the people like me were.

After I came out at twenty three, I decided it was time to create stories I couldn't find at Waldenbooks. If there weren't many gay characters in my favorite genres, I would reimagine them myself, populating them with men who loved men. I would subvert them and remake them to my own ends. And if I was lucky enough, someone else would want to read them.

My friends say my brain works a little differently - I sees relationships between things that others miss, and get more done in a day than most folks manage in a week. Although I was born an introvert, I learned to reach outside himself and connect with others like me.

I write stories that subvert expectations, and transform sci fi, fantasy, and contemporary worlds into something new and unexpected. I run both Queer Sci Fi and QueeRomance Ink with Mark, sites that bring people like us together to promote and celebrate fiction that reflects us.

I was recognized as one of the top new gay authors in the 2017 Rainbow Awards, and my debut novel "Skythane" received two awards. In 2019, I won Rainbow Awards for three other books, and became full member of the Science Fiction and Fantasy Writers of America in 2020.

My writing, whether queer romance or genre fiction (or a little bit of both) brings LGBTQ+ energy to my stories, infusing them with love, beauty and power and making them soar. I imagine a world that *could be*, and in the process, maybe changes the world that is just a little.

ALSO BY J. SCOTT COATSWORTH

Oberon Cycle:

Skythane | Lander | Ithani (Dec 2020)

Liminal Sky:

The Stark Divide | The Rising Tide | The Shoreless Sea

Other Sci Fi/Fantasy:

The Autumn Lands | Cailleadhama | The Great North | Homecoming |
The Last Run | Spells & Stardust Anthology | Wonderland

Contemporary/Magical Realism:

Between the Lines (rereleasing 2021) | I Only Want to Be With You |
Flames (rereleasing June 2021) | The River City Chronicles | Slow Thaw

99¢ Shorts:

Chinatown | Eventide | Translation

LIKE WHAT YOU JUST READ?

I thought I would share the first chapters from two of my other novellas - "The Last Run" and "Cailleadhama."
Hope you enjoy them!

CHAPTER ONE - THE LAST RUN

Sera's back arched as she gulped a lungful of air, her eyes bulging out of their sockets. She collapsed back on the memory foam of her sleep pod, sucking oxygen into her lungs gratefully.

It was a bit stale, but not immediately fatal—a good sign given how they escaped near-certain destruction by the skin of their teeth, as Earth and her local colonies fell into chaos and self-imposed destruction.

Sera's throat was raw, dry—the antiseptic spray either hadn't worked or hadn't been administered by the *Spin Diver's* wake-up protocols. "Waaaater."

A slim white feeder line slipped down from above to mouth level. She took the sipper between her lips and sucked in the gloriously wet liquid.

Like the air, it tasted a bit off. She sighed. *Time enough to figure that out later.*

She drank her fill and sat up, swinging her feet off the edge of the couch to look around the sleep room.

The other three pods were dark.

"Tavi!" Sera slipped off the couch and winced. Every one of her muscles ached.

She hobbled her way to the closest pod. *Please—no.*

It felt like just minutes before—when their fingers had been intertwined, Tavi giving her a quick kiss as the ship shuddered all around them, the air filling with noxious smoke. Staring at each other as the hardened plas lids slid closed over them.

Sera fumbled with the manual release controls on Tavi's pod, frantic. They were unresponsive, as dark as the pod itself.

Sera stumbled to the wall and retrieved the axe that was strapped there for emergencies. She managed to lift it up, her shoulder muscles on fire from the weight. She brought it down blade-first on the plas cover of the dark sleep pod. The reinforced plas cracked but didn't break.

She lifted the axe again and brought it down hard on the slick surface.

The axe blade skittered across the smooth shell, and the handle slipped out of her grasp. The axe fell on the metallic floor on the far side of the pod with a loud clatter in the deceleration-created gravity.

Sera squeezed past the pod to retrieve it, sparing a quick glance for the two unoccupied pods.

Jace and Herrol hadn't even made it to the ship. They were long dead by now.

Sera lifted the axe once more and brought it down on the cover with all her weakened strength.

The plas shattered at last, revealing the pod's contents.

The musky smell of decay slammed into Sera, driving her back toward the exit hatch. She couldn't believe that it was true—that Tavi was long dead, her corpse a shrunken mess of bones and dried flesh.

"Oh God." Sera stumbled backward and slammed her hand on

the hatch release. She practically fell through it, slamming her hand on the door control outside.

It spiraled closed, shutting off the horrible sight, but leaving the sickly-sweet smell lingering in the air.

Sera fell to her knees and retched.

After almost twenty-five years in suspension, there was nothing left in her to come out, but still her stomach heaved. It was a primal reaction, far beyond her ability to control. *She's gone.*

Then she just lay there, wrecked and broken. "Tavi." *How did this happen?*

Time slowed and dilated.

Her mind refused to process what she had just seen. It was too visceral, too real.

Too painful.

She closed her eyes and sobbed.

Jas'Aya stood up and straightened, rubbing her back where the muscles knotted and ached from the hard work in the field.

Around her, the purple rows of hencha plants stretched out into the distance, their red stalks moving of their own accord even when there was no breeze.

Her shoulder sack was full of hencha berries teased from the semi-sentient plant—red, orange and blue spheres that emitted the most delicious scent.

If she closed her eyes, she could almost hear the murmuring of the plants. They spoke to one another, whispers that drifted tantalizingly out of reach. She wished she could understand what they were saying. Sometimes she felt like she got a word or two, but then it slipped away on the wind that blew steadily up the valley from the Harkness Sea.

She had stopped telling people about her little fantasies. The last time she had mentioned them, she'd gotten in trouble with her shift supervisor and had been put on probation for a week. To the rest of the crew, the hencha were just plants.

Jas dusted off her light blue skirt, the kind all the field workers wore. She needed a break, even if it was just a short one. She pulled her unusually dark hair back behind her ears and set off toward the collector.

The sun was bright green overhead, matched to a sky which was a deeper shade of the same color. It was already past noon—soon they'd be called in for lunch under the welcoming shade of one of the big-leaved flop trees that dotted the plantation.

She was thirsty. It was warm out today and she'd been chewing on a piece of bacca root all morning long to keep her mouth wet. She spat it out—it was reduced to a black, well-gummed wad.

Jas dropped her load of berries into the collector, which hummed happily as it processed them by type.

She waved at Meriam two rows over and took a sip of water from the collector's spigot. It was warm but welcome as it washed away the dust of the farm.

She was ahead of quota—she had a way with the hencha, which responded to her more readily than to most of the other harvesters. If she kept at it, she might earn a bonus day she could spend with her mother at home. Lyn'Aya was sick. Jas didn't know what was wrong with her but it seemed serious—the skin on her arms had strange bumps, and her fingernails were covered with red lines. Her joints ached too—she hardly ever managed a full night's sleep anymore—and her nose bled whenever she sneezed.

Some of the other older women had the same symptoms, but no one seemed to know why.

If she could have, Jas would have stayed at home to care for Lyn'Aya, to keep her as comfortable as possible.

Her mother was a formidable person, stocky and forceful. She had clawed her way up from serfdom to contractor after Jas had been born and she'd shared all she had learned about their world with her daughter.

Jas returned to the next plant in the row. She knelt, ripping out a heyfa weed that had wrapped itself around the base of the plant. The little yellow thing screamed and twisted in her hand before fading to a pale white and going limp.

She threw it down on the ground and stomped on it until it was flat.

She knelt before the plant and her fingers worked quickly, slipping through the red leaves of the hencha to find the bundle of nerves underneath. Her fingers massaged them gently, and she felt it shiver under her touch.

Silanya. The word slipped into her mind, the name of this particular hencha plant, as closely as she could translate it into the human tongue. They often spoke to her when she harvested their berries, though she didn't always understand them.

Jas'Aya.

Thank you. It wasn't in human words so much as a feeling, a warmth that spread through her mind like the opening of a flower.

Jas felt a shiver of pleasure in the hencha's nerves, both a physical and mental sensation. Then the plant's skin split and a few berries were deposited in her open hand.

She didn't know if the hencha spoke to anyone else. It felt private, something special she shared with the strange alien life form. She was afraid to speak of it to anyone else, lest she be penalized again for her "strange ideas."

She pulled her hand out gently and deposited the berries in her bag. "Thank you."

The hencha rustled as if in reply.

"They're coming!" Cyr's voice carried down the rows of hencha as she ran toward them, the woman's long blond hair flying behind her, her arms waving wildly in the air. "They're coming!"

The women gathered around her as she arrived. Cyr was sweating and out of breath, hands on her knees.

"Who's coming?" Jas had never seen the woman get so worked up.

"Runners from Earth." She grinned, "There's gonna be a Market Day in Gullytown!"

Hours later, as the sun dropped toward the horizon, Jas dumped the last of the berries into the collector impatiently, tapping her foot while it sorted the load.

Market Day. The words carried a bit of magic, like a fairy tale that parents told their children that would never actually come true. Still, she wanted to believe in it. The last one had been before she was born, but her mother had told her about it:

The big ships come in with all manner of wonderful items—spices, fabrics and flitter parts and raw materials and medicines that will cure almost anything. There are machines big and small, wondrous dishes and toys and things you never dreamed of. Her mother's eyes had glittered in the firelight, and Jas had imagined buying herself wings from the Runners. Gauzy fairy wings that would carry her wherever she wanted to go.

The runs arrived about once every two decades. This one was already a couple years overdue, but no one seemed to know how they chose their schedules.

Some of her friends had whispered that there would be no more of them, that Earth had surely forgotten her colonies, including little agrarian Tharassas. Some—the Separatists—wished they would never come back at all.

Jas had been entranced by all the stories. There was something amazing and romantic about the idea of traveling between the stars, of traversing the vast distances between planets like modern-day pirates.

Mamma had told her stories about the pirates on the Seven Seas, back on Earth—Lon Jon Siller, the Black Bard…

And now a ship was coming and there would be another Market Day!

"You're a little off today." Jemmy, her supervisor, frowned at the totals on the side of the collector.

"Sorry… I've been sick." *More like daydreaming about Market Day.*

Jemmy nodded. "Just don't let it happen again."

"I won't. Listen…" She put her hand on Jemmy's arm. "I need a day off. Just one."

His bushy brows furrowed. "I don't know. We're in the middle of the harvest. I need you here—"

"It's my mother," she lied. Lyn'Aya *was* sick, but Jas had more on her mind than a day at home. "She's taken a turn for the worse." She looked over her shoulder at the rows of hencha. "I think mamma's close to seed."

Jemmy bit his lip. Hencha plants died when they went to seed. Everyone knew it. "All right. One day. But I need you back here on Martasday."

"Thank you." She threw her arms around him. "You don't know how much this means." She kissed his cheek.

He snorted. "Enough of that. See you day after tomorrow."

Jemmy was a bit skittish about touching, but she couldn't help herself. She was going to Market Day for her mother! "Thank you!" She practically ran to the flit stop, but even though the flitter was there, she had to wait for the others to finish before it could take her home.

The women—blond every last one but her—boarded the little craft, and its rotors spun to lift it silently into the air.

They had long since stopped noticing her differences.

The flitter swerved off to the south toward Corinth, the village where she and the others in her crew lived. The tiny village sat up in the hills, looking over the wide valley where the hencha plantations thrived.

Jas had worked in them all. Each plant could only be harvested once every twenty days, so the workforce continually rotated through the various owners' fields. The plantation owners paid the supervisors and some of that pay—a very small amount—trickled down into her account.

A breeze blew up from Gullytown, making the hencha below sway like a red sea. Even up here, she could smell the plants—they had a bright, sharp, sweet scent that got into her hair and clothing, and had to be washed out at home, but she didn't mind.

The flitter swooped low over the fields, and then caught a warm updraft and soared up into the hills.

"Wish I could go to Gullytown for the Market Day." Myr'Oyl stared off into the distance, down the valley toward the capital. The sun was setting over the ridges there, painting the clouds green and gold.

"Ever been?"

Myr nodded. "I was ten the last time. My papa took me—it took three days to get there on urseback."

"My mamma went before I was born." *Three days to get to Gullytown!* Jas needed a faster way.

Cyr had said the Runners were already inbound. Market Day would likely be in the next day or two. Even if it lasted a week, all the good trade would be gone.

She had an idea. It was a little crazy, and she'd miss more than one day at work, but she was sure she could sweet-talk Jemmy out of a penalty when she returned.

The flitter slipped out of the sky to alight just below the hilltop where the twenty small cottages that made up Corinth perched overlooking the valley. The other women dismounted one by one, heading off to their own homes.

Jas waved farewell to the other field hands. She held back, waiting until they were all gone. "Torry. A moment?" She rested a hand on his shoulder, aware of her impact on him even if she didn't feel the same.

The flitter pilot nodded, running a hand through his blond hair. "What's up?"

"I need a favor."

CHAPTER ONE - CAILLEADHAMA

Colton sat at the old, salvaged mirror in his wreck of an apartment, high above the Main Street Canal on San Francisco's drowned waterfront. Not that San Francisco didn't have its pride. As the Capital of Pacifica, she was still a center of commerce and politics.

But canal rats like Colton didn't matter much anymore.

The bed behind him, salvaged from another abandoned apartment, was a mess of sheets, a reminder of the trick he'd brought home the night before, someone who'd been paid enough to overlook Colton's shortcomings.

Colton took out a vial of testosterone—his last one, bought at a dear price from the Pharmacist. He pulled out a clean syringe and took off the plastic top, pulling out the stopper to 5 milliliters. He inserted the needle into the bottle, and pushed the air in, an act familiar to him from long practice. Then he pulled out the last of the drug, flicking the syringe twice and pushing out all the air bubbles.

He replaced the needle with a smaller gauge, dumping the larger one into an old caramel corn can he kept for his medical waste.

He used a piece of cotton and a bottle of cheap liquor to wipe down the injection site on his thigh, sterilizing it as best he could. Once it was dry, he took a deep breath, pinching his muscle and pulling his skin to the side. He inserted the needle into his leg, drawing the syringe back a bit to make sure there was no blood. He had to be careful to avoid injecting the hormone directly into his bloodstream.

It hurt a little, but he was used to it.

He dumped the used syringe and the empty vial into the can. He had friends who weren't so careful to use clean needles, for their hormones or recreational drugs. Some of those friends were now dead, or worse.

Next, he took the medical bandages that he carefully washed every day, and wrapped them around his chest, binding his breasts tightly.

He didn't look at them. He hated those reminders of his female body—he'd been running from that accident of birth for years.

He wrapped the bandages around himself three or four times, holding in his breath. Once he had his breasts secured, he adjusted them to the side to make his chest as flat as possible.

He looked at the results in the mirror. It would have to do.

He wished he could afford to be re-sequenced. To truly make his body match his gender, to not feel counterfeit in his own form.

Colton glanced out through the broken window. The lights of the City were starting to come on over there as dusk approached. He lived in a no man's land, the part of the City where the water encroaching from the Bay had reached the old first and second floors. Toward the heart of the City, on the other side of the Wall, the rich still carried on as if nothing had changed.

Those with money called the drowned parts of the city the Canal District. It ran from the old Levis Plaza down to China Basin along the City's Bay side. There were a number of tony restaurants on the roofs and higher floors of the City behind the Wall that offered views of this supposedly "romantic" neighborhood. For a fee, you could even take a ride through the ruins on a gondola.

That was Colton's "day job". It brought in enough money to afford food, hormones, and little else, at least, when he was able to pay Mason his overdue boat storage fees.

So at night, he haunted the drowned streets, looking for those he could help, or sometimes relieve of their excess cash.

It was time to get going. The hours between 6 p.m. and midnight were his prime business time. If he could make enough money shaking down tourists that night, he might be able to get his gondola out of hock. But he had to visit the Pharmacist first.

He pulled on an old Pier 39 sweatshirt and a pair of jeans. He slapped on his white data-band, and grabbed the portable solar array, which provided his apartment with a small trickle of power, from its place on the windowsill, stuffing it into the old ventilator shaft, and setting the grill back over the opening to cover it. It was a less than ideal hiding place, but better than nothing.

Colton closed the door behind him and locked it with the heavy iron lock and key he'd traded for—nothing high tech but it would keep out the casual vandal.

He took the steps three at a time, descending quickly toward the third floor. About halfway down, he ran into one of his neighbors, Morgan, who lived on the fifth floor. Morgan was a thirty-year-old systems engineer who had fled the City under a cloud of embezzlement charges.

"Hey, Morgan," Colton said, hoping his breasts were masked well enough. He hated the thought that others might see them, might think he was a woman. Especially when he had a crush on someone.

Morgan nodded as they passed one another, but said nothing.

Colton frowned. He knew Morgan was gay—he'd seen some of

the city boys who came home with him for a little Canal District adventure. But with Colton, there was no chemistry. Nothing.

He continued on down the stairs to the third floor. The building had been a University Extension campus at one point. Now it was filled to the gills with those who couldn't afford living space inside the Wall—some employed, some out of work, some plying the gray areas of the law—the lower dregs of society.

The buildings of the Canal District were surrounded with floating debris, much of it placed there on purpose to provide a sort of sidewalk allowing transit from building to building. These varied from floating rafts and platforms to zip lines and old rooflines, all connected into a makeshift passage from one block to the next, above the dark water.

Some of the braver of the City youth from behind the Wall would come out there on a dare late at night, exploring the dangerous district with their friends. And if Colton happened to liberate them from their money, maybe that would teach them to stay out of the Canals.

Then again, maybe not. Nothing much ever seemed to change there.

Colton climbed out the broken window frame on the building's old third floor, out onto the floating sidewalk, stepping lightly from raft to wooden boat to platform along the front of the building, his feet finding firm footing with the ease of long practice.

He barely spared a glance for the Main Street Wall that ran along the far side of the street, holding back the sea.

One day it, too, would fall, and the rich bastards on the other side would see what it felt like to live in a drowned city.

He'd learned over the last two years what spots to avoid—which parts were solid and which would drop you into the dirty Bay water that coursed through the streets below.

Colton reached the end of the block—the old signs for Main

and Mission still hung just above the water level, the traffic lights now a nesting place for pigeons.

He pulled a piece of metal rebar fashioned into a makeshift handle out of his pocket, and placed it on the zip line slung between the two buildings. Gripping the duct tape handles with practiced ease, he swung over the Canal, landing neatly on the wide I-beam on the other side. This building had been under construction when the floods had come, and now stood a rusting and hollow shell.

This part of the City was deep in shadow, even though the sun was just setting on the other side of the peninsula. He jumped from beam to beam, pivoting around upright support columns, and reached the old Fed Building that took up the other half of the block.

A hand reached out of the darkness from one of the windows of the granite structure. Colton grasped it by the wrist without thinking, swinging his back against the building and pulling his assailant out the open window. The assailant splashed into the water below.

"Don't fuck with me," he called after whoever it was, and continued along without a backward glance.

He was a big enough guy that people usually didn't mess with him, but pith-addled junkies had no sense.

At Market, he turned right and climbed up to the series of concrete planters that fronted the Fed Building. Once thirty feet above street level, they were now islands, connected by heavy wooden boards.

Ahead he could see the glow of the night market on the top floor of the half-drowned Ferry Building. A place where you could buy almost anything. Or anyone.

He reached the end of the Fed Building just as the sun was setting behind him. To the north, he could just make out the Island of Alcatraz. Somewhere beyond that, around the curve of the peninsula, was the ancient Golden Gate Bridge. Once a beacon of hope, or so his mother had told him. Now the Tube ferried the rich and well-heeled across it to and from the walled enclave of the Marin Peninsula. Colton imagined he could see the guards on the far side of the Bay patrolling the Seawall, keeping poor saps like him out. Except when the rich needed to have their lawns trimmed or their furniture polished. Or their vital organs replaced.

He sighed.

Floating next to the base of the old Southern Pacific Building at the foot of the Market Street Canal was a wooden pier, the launching point for the ferry to the Night Market. Colton swiped his data-band across the ferryman's, slitting a credit to the man's account. The ferryman gestured him onto the boat. The ferry would take him across the black waters to the Night Market. *Like the River Styx.*

He'd made this journey many times before, but always somewhat warily. The Night Market wasn't a place for the innocent or undefended. He patted the T-Whip tucked under his shirt, hidden inside the bandages where he could easily access it, at need. It gave him a small sense of comfort.

He was out of T. He hoped the Pharmacist would see him tonight, and that her price was not too high.

The ferryman untied the little wooden boat and cast off, rowing them slowly across the drowned plaza below, toward the Ferry Building. As they approached, he looked back at the City; she was still a beautiful thing, perhaps haunted now, covered in a veil of darkened buildings, the lights shining from behind like the glow of a halo.

After a few minutes, he reached the landing. It was showtime.

www.ingramcontent.com/pod-product-compliance
Lightning Source LLC
Chambersburg PA
CBHW071839190726
48292CB00005B/1834